THE MOUNTAIN THAT WALKED

KATHERINE HOLUBITSKY

ORCA BOOK PUBLISHERS

National Library of Canada Cataloguing in Publication Data

ISBN 1-55143-392-3 (bound).—ISBN 1-55143-376-1 (pbk.)

1. Frank (Alta.)—History—Landslide, 1903—Juvenile fiction.
I. Title.

PS8565.O645M69 2005   jC813'.54   C2005-900063-5

Library of Congress Control Number: 2004118006

Summary: The year is 1903, and Charlie, on the run from false accusations, ends up in Frank, a coal-mining town about to experience disaster.

Orca Book Publishers gratefully acknowledges the support for its publishing programs provided by the following agencies: the Government of Canada through the Book Publishing Industry Development Program (BPIDP), the Canada Council for the Arts, and the British Columbia Arts Council.

Design and typesetting: John van der Woude
Cover artwork: Leslie Elizabeth Watts
Printed and bound in Canada

Orca Book Publishers
Box 5626 Station B
Victoria, BC Canada
V8R 6S4

Orca Book Publishers
PO Box 468
Custer, WA USA
98240-0468

09 08 07 06 05 • 6 5 4 3 2 1

for my parents, Don and Mary James

At first Matthew suggested getting a "Home" boy. But I said "no" flat to that. "They may be all right—I'm not saying they're not—but no London street arabs for me," I said. "Give me a native born at least. There'll be a risk, no matter who we get. But I'll feel easier in my mind and sleep sounder at nights if we get a born Canadian."

—Marilla Cuthbert
Anne of Green Gables (1908)

One

March 22, 1903

I burrow deeper into my straw tick. Drifting between sleep and wakefulness, I pull the tangle of rags tight beneath my chin, feeling chilled to my very toes. Suddenly I open my eyes. It strikes me there's no glow coming from the room below me, and the smell of dying ashes hangs heavy in the air. The old mantelpiece clock strains—warning its intention to strike. It tolls out seven long chimes. Blimey! I sit bolt upright. They'll whip me for lying in so late and letting the fire go out! I listen closer, but I don't hear anybody moving in the cabin below. If I'm quick, I still might have a chance to get the fire stoked before anyone discovers it's out.

The wind has blown a fine layer of snow through the cracks in the roof during the night. I throw my rags off and, shivering, dust snow from my hair. I'm already wearing both jumpers I own, as well as the jacket the home provided me. Quick as I can, I pull on my second pair of britches, nearly to the middle of my calves now, and, willing my fingers to quit trembling, I button them up.

I don't weigh a lot for my age. This is because the Brooks brothers don't feed me much more than scraps: peelings, bread crusts and porridge so thin it can be drunk from a cup. Still, the ladder complains as I start to make my way down. I wince. The last thing I want is to advertise my late appearance. But I still don't hear anyone stirring, so I continue to climb down to the main floor from the loft.

It's unusually quiet—there's no snoring coming from the back of the cabin. This reminds me that Buck Brooks stayed the night in Macleod. Albert's all I need worry about, but I'm not much comforted by the thought because I know from experience that Albert is the one I have to most worry about. Of the two of them, he requires the least excuse to reach for the buggy whip. I stoke wood into the fire and poke it back to life. All the time I look over my shoulder in case Albert should be creeping up on me, waiting to lick me for being so late. Once the fire is snapping, I steal just a moment to rub my hands together to take off the chill.

The fire grows brighter, illuminating the further corners of the cabin. I creep quiet as I can to Albert's bed and reach beneath it for the chamber pot. It's my chore to empty the foul pots in the morning. In the dim light, I can't see Albert for his mound of bedclothes. I think again how silent he is. He likes his whiskey, and when he finally passes out, most of the night he gurgles and snorts like a man drowning in his own drink.

I step into my shoes where I'd left them parked by the door. They're beat up quite badly now; a few months back I'd split the ends to give my toes a place to go. As far as I can figure, I'm about sixteen—it could be I'm even nearer to seventeen. Not a boy anymore, but a lad. I'm still thin, like I said, not filled out, but that hasn't stopped me from sprouting upward. I've never owned a pair of overshoes, so before I leave the cabin I tie strips of gunny sack around the bare part of my legs to protect them from the bite of snow.

I can't see through the window panes for hoarfrost, and I have to tug hard to free the cabin door. For nearly two weeks, the temperature has hovered about twenty-five degrees below zero and everything is frozen, off-kilter and rigid. I swear I won't ever get used to a place so sullen and cold.

Standing on the stoop, I gaze at the clouds of ice crystals hanging low in the early morning sky. With my first breath, the hairs in my nose freeze instantly. I pinch the bridge to warm it up, then step off the stoop into six inches of powdery new snow. Carrying the tin chamber pot, I plunge forward toward the outhouse.

I'm not ten feet from the stoop when my foot runs aground on something unfamiliar and I stumble. I manage to keep my balance, but what's in the pot splashes into the snow. In the thin morning light, I stare at the snow and the yellow patch where the liquid is trickling into it. Something black lies beneath. I rub the spot with my foot. It's a boot—I recognize it as belonging to Albert Brooks.

At first, I don't think much of it. It could be the boot became stuck in the snow, and Old Man Brooks in his drunkenness continued walking and left it there. But on closer inspection it appears to stick out at an odd angle. Something makes me brush more snow away. A leg clad in denim is attached to the boot. I squat on my haunches, set the chamber pot aside and brusquely brush snow off the lump in front of me. I jump back, thinking I'm seeing things, when Albert Brooks's back appears. I stand up, turn away and try to blink my mind blank. I turn back. The apparition hasn't changed.

"Mr. Brooks!" I roll the body of the old drunk over. His blue eyes, frozen open, fix on the navy sky. The hand-kerchief knotted about his neck is stiff, and his grizzled beard flops to his chest, a heavy chunk of ice. I've never seen anyone so dead and so completely frozen. "So that's why I didn't hear you snoring," I say aloud.

I don't jump up and down or start shrieking. It's not that I'm cold-hearted. Even Albert—if he was somehow watching—wouldn't be surprised at how little sadness I have at finding him dead. He must have known that he and Buck had whipped anything akin to affection I might have developed for them right out of me. Neither of them had shown a soft spot toward me in the nearly three years I'd been in Macleod.

I'd heard of fellows getting turned around in a white-out; blizzards can whip up fast, confusing a person's sense of direction. I'd heard stories of men returning from tending their animals, found frozen to death within yards of their cabin door. And those were sober ones. It could have been that, or it could have been Albert died of a stopped heart.

The tears begin welling up, blurring the hard lines of Albert's corpse. But they're not prompted by his passing so much as the thought of how helpless I feel at being stuck in this lonesome place. Then a worse thought comes to me. I think of Buck, and my mind freezes along with everything else. Buck will come home in a few hours and find his brother dead! He'll think I'm responsible. It doesn't matter if Albert got caught in a blizzard or how he met his end. I was here alone with him, and Buck won't give me a chance to explain.

Thinking through things as quick as I can, I determine the best thing to do is observe from a hiding place how Buck reacts. Depending on his reaction, I'll make up my mind what to do from there. I brush the rest of the snow from Albert's body so Buck can flat out see him on the way to the cabin. His left hand still clutches the whiskey bottle he couldn't let go of, even in death.

I then return to the cabin, where I pocket my copy of *The Pilgrim's Progress* as well as the buck knife I'd come across in the dirt outside the Winnipeg Home. I'm already wearing every piece of clothing I own, but I'll be needing something to eat.

It's not easy being a thief when it isn't natural in you. I'd long ago discovered that. But the circumstances don't leave me much choice. I find a bit of cheese, half a loaf of bread and a tin of beef in the pantry. I wrap them in the flour sacks I'd stitched together for bedclothes. With the sky brightening around me, I dart toward the barn. On the way, I brush over my footprints with a spruce branch so my tracks don't distract Buck from Albert's body. When this is done, I climb the rickety ladder into the hayloft. From here I can lay low and look out the small square window into the yard.

It's nearly two hours before I hear the clip-clop of the dapple grays. Buck is coming up the trail in the cutter. I stay crouched, lying still in the straw as he stables the horses below me in the barn. He curses when he finds there's no fresh water to give the animals. With what's happened, I've neglected to do my chores. It's up to me to break the ice, get the pump working each morning and tote water to the livestock. I feel bad for a moment, not on account of Buck, but for the cattle and pigs that depend on me and are down there waiting expectantly in their pens.

After hearing Buck leave the barn, I watch him come into view through the window. He makes his way toward the cabin. His woolly head turns, noting something isn't right. I can sense his puzzlement—he's angry noticing the chores aren't done. He stops walking altogether, his black eyes riveted on the chimney. There's no smoke rising out of it, because my fire has died down again. Buck starts up again, walking quicker the more furious he gets with me. He comes upon Albert's body in the snow.

His holler echoes in the frigid air, and I'm sure every farmer within fifty miles has heard it. He bends down and starts clawing and smacking Albert—attempting to raise his brother, until he realizes that Albert's just lying there taking it, with no intention of fighting back. Buck finally stands up. "Charlie Sutherland!"

There's nothing unusual in Buck using both my names. They always refer to me as Charlie Sutherland—it's "Charlie Sutherland, where have you got to?! Charlie Sutherland, have you cleaned the pig pen yet? Charlie Sutherland, you haven't got time to go to school, and don't let us catch you sneakin' off neither. We didn't take you in and house and feed you so's you could just goof off." It's never just Charlie. It's as if I'm a breed of something, and unless they use both my names I won't be a breed anymore, but a regular human being.

"Charlie Sutherland! What have you done to Albert?!"

Buck is wheezing as he hollers, twisting and turning, working himself into a frightful frenzy. His temples swell up the way they always do when he gets himself in a rage. I lower my head in case, in his jerking around, his eyes sweep up to the window in the hayloft.

"You finally gone and done it to Albert! I saw it coming in you, you filthy cur!"

I know as soon as I hear him blaming me like that—I have to get out of here as quick as possible. Before Buck starts scouring the farm.

I peek out the window again. Buck is struggling to move Albert's body, trying to get hold of him beneath the arms. He can't budge him—the corpse is unwieldy and too heavy for him to haul anywhere by himself. Buck turns and marches toward the barn. I duck. He can't *know* I'm in the hayloft! I wait. My heart is thumping so loud I'm sure Buck will hear it, if he doesn't see me first. But he doesn't say a word when he enters the barn. All I can hear is his crying and snuffling as he rummages around looking for something. He must have found what he's after because he leaves again. Cautiously, I lift myself up on my elbows and peer out the window. Buck pulls a wooden sled over to where Albert is laid out. He bends, and after lifting the top half of the body onto the sled, he hauls Albert's corpse toward the cabin. The weight of the body and the boots dragging out behind it leave two channels in the snow. After wrestling Albert into the cabin, Buck closes the door.

I have very little time. I clamber down the ladder faster than a chicken skittering from a hatchet. I tear out the barn door and race down the road with my bundle of rags hung on my shoulder like a rucksack. I'm soon breathing heavily. Cold air rushes into my lungs, and I imagine them freezing solid and me not being able to draw in another breath. I have an idea that I'll run to Tillie's. If I can get her alone, I can explain what's happened. If she can't help me, I know she'll at least help me figure out what to do. Tillie Carson lives five miles down Willow Creek. She's the one person who's shown me any kindness since I arrived in Macleod.

Despite the new layer of snow, the trail is passable, since Buck's just run over it. Still, I muck in my footsteps with the horses' hoofprints so my path won't be clear. I'm chilled through to my core by the time Carsons' chimney comes into view. The sight and smell of wood smoke is welcoming, and it gets stronger as I near Tillie's farm. I hide around the corner of the barn at first, my eyes scuttling over the yard like a common thief's. But there's no one working outside, and my fingers and toes are so cold they've turned into fleshy lumps. They do nothing but get in my way as I try to adjust my makeshift rucksack. It's hard to be sure if your mind is sharp enough to make important decisions when you can't even get your body parts to do what you want. If I'm to come up with a decent plan for what to do next, I've got to get myself warmed up.

As silently as I can, I open the barn door. For a moment, I listen. Except for the pawing and whinnying of the Carsons' horses, I don't hear any voices. I creep into the building, tiptoeing past two milk cows in their stalls and around the haymow—a big hump of loose hay piled in the center of the floor. I duck into the room where the feed grain is stored. The ceiling is much lower here than in the rest of the barn. Walls, almost to the rafters, divide the room into four large bins filled waist-deep with grain. Jumping into the first bin, I splash oats over my legs and arms until I'm immersed right up to my neck. The dust I rouse floats in streaks of sunlight, and husks fly about, clinging to my hair. Slowly, a slight tingling comes back into my fingers and toes.

I've just got the feeling back when I hear horses on the trail. A voice hollers out, bringing the team to a stop. A door slams and more voices; I guess it's Mr. Carson greeting a visitor. I can't decipher what's being said except that the visitor is talking and shouting faster than most can listen. A terrible worry strikes me, and I sneak out of the oat bin and over to a crack where the light shines through the boards in the barn wall. I peer out. Just as I feared, it's Buck Brooks. He's ranting about what's happened, trying to get through to Mr. Carson about his misfortune. Mr. Carson is having a hard time making sense of what he's saying, although the words "cold-blooded murderer" and "filthy low-down Home boy" are coming out loud and clear. Mr. Carson tries to get him to speak slower. Eventually, all the racket brings Mrs. Carson, Tillie, her brother, Jesse, and their farmhand, John, to the door.

"Charlie?" I hear Mrs. Carson say, not believing. "Charlie murdered Albert? Oh, Buck, that can't be right."

When I hear that, I want to run right across the barnyard and hug her. But I know that would be a mistake because it would still be my word against Buck's. And Buck isn't about to call his poor dead brother a mean old drunkard who was so dumb-headed he wandered blind into a blizzard in the middle of the night. Even though everybody knows he'd be perfectly capable, and they wouldn't be overwhelmed with surprise.

But Buck has another purpose that others aren't likely to know. It's an easy way for him to get rid of me without paying my wages. The Brooks brothers were supposed to begin paying me a wage for my labors once I turned fourteen, but I haven't seen one penny in those two years. By accusing me of murder, Buck could get rid of me and the debt he owes me. He could then go and get himself another boy from the Home, one who isn't worn out and starved half to death. The Home is sure to be obliging once he convinces them they'd saddled him with a convict the first time around.

I have to put it out of my mind until I can get Tillie alone.

Mr. Carson and Jesse climb onto the cutter next to Buck— I guess they're off to take a firsthand look at Albert. Tillie, her mother, and John return to the cabin. I sit down on the straw next to the crack in the boards where I can keep an eye on things. It's warm enough in the barn with the heat from the two cows. Four workhorses are also stabled along the wall across from me.

About an hour later I hear the cabin door open again. I peer through the crack to see John standing on the stoop, adjusting the flaps of his cap over his ears. He strolls into the yard, where he grabs a pitchfork from where it leans against the woodpile. He continues up toward the barn. I glance quickly around for a hiding place. I could easily disappear beneath the haymow, but, considering he's carrying a pitchfork, I reason that might be a poor choice. I sneak over to where the plow and other implements are stored and crouch behind them. Moments later the door opens, and with the sun behind him, John's shadow stretches across the floor. This makes him look about a hundred feet tall. But he's really only a chap of regular height, thick through the chest, with the hair on his face trimmed into muttonchops. Raising the pitchfork, he walks over to the haymow, where he spears a great wad of hay. My stomach takes a tumble just watching him drive into it. John carries the pitchfork full of hay over to the cows. He then proceeds to feed the horses—filling their buckets with oats and splashing fresh water into their troughs.

Sounds carry a long way in the cold air, and I notice John's head turn at the same time as I hear the return of Buck's cutter. It draws into the farmyard, and again I hear people emerge from the cabin. John leaves the barn to meet them.

"It's true!" Jesse explodes with the news. "Mr. Brooks—he's dead, alright!"

"Jesse." Mr. Carson attempts to hush his boy.

But Jesse isn't much more than twelve and can't restrain himself. "Dead and lying in the cabin, stiffer than the table he's laid across!"

Mr. Carson repeats Jesse's name, quite sharply this time.

I can't hear what's said next—it sounds rather like the cooing of the doves in the rafters above me—but I gather it must be Mrs. Carson extending her sympathies to Buck.

"Yes, well, thank you, ma'am. But what's important now is to get the little bastard that done this."

This is immediately followed by a small, familiar cracking sound. I scramble back to the crack in the boards. Sure enough, Buck is loading his Winchester, preparing to hunt me down.

Two

"Now, Buck," Mr. Carson attempts to soothe him. "I know he's your brother, but let's try and approach this with a level head. I can't say I saw any marks on the body to outright convict Charlie. Let's try to find the boy and talk to him first."

"Course there weren't any marks," Buck retorts. "He was too smart for that. He waited until Albert was out the door and he locked it behind him. What he wasn't smart about was to know that I'd figure out what he'd done. From the time he came to live with us, that one was full of the devil. Brought his natural inherited wickedness from the streets where he came. Albert did what he could to chase it out of him, but, as you can see, his efforts were of no use." Buck climbs back into the cutter. "I'm going back there and I'm going to flush him out. I know that little weasel, he'll only be curled up in the straw somewhere." He pats the barrel of the rifle.

It's a thought as evil as he's made me out to be, but I wish it would accidentally go off.

"Haw!" Buck wheels the team around and starts toward the farm.

"Buck!" Mr. Carson calls after him. A cloud of frosty air drifts from his mouth along with his words. "John and I are going into town for the Mounted Police. If you find Charlie, just hold your temper. We'll be back as quick as we can."

John steps forward. He also calls after Buck's receding figure. "He's right, Buck. We know what you're feeling, but there's no point making things worse than they already are. One corpse is plenty enough, let's don't make it two."

Mr. Carson and John are now hurrying toward the barn for their horses. I dash into the granary, where I dive back into the bin of oats. I can hear the commotion as they hitch the horses to the sleigh. While they work, I consider going out and explaining that I had nothing to do with Albert Brooks's death. I even climb out of the bin and stand just by the doorway, trying to gather the nerve. From their conversation with Buck, I gather they'd be willing to stand up for me. Still, I hesitate. I guess I'm more afraid that without a lawman around, Buck's gun will argue louder and quicker than the two of them possibly could.

"He could have done it." It's John's voice. "It could be that Albert drove him to it. Maybe he just whipped him one too many times."

"Maybe so," Mr. Carson answers. "But I don't think so. I can't believe that Charlie is the murdering kind."

"Well, I wouldn't have thought so either. But you never know what a person will do when their life depends on it. Anyway, even if he did it to save his own skin, it'll make no difference. They'll hang him just the same. It's Buck's word against his. A poor Home boy with no kin won't ever stand a chance."

I don't hear Mr. Carson's answer as they drive off.

That's it. There's no showing myself now. I creep back into the bin. Even after I hear the sleigh jangling down the road, my mind keeps repeating what John said. Even if I didn't do it, they'll *hang* me just the same.

I stay crouched in the bin, knowing I have no hope of staying at the Carsons'. I have to get as far away as I can. I have to tell Tillie. I have to tell her first so she knows I'm not a murderer—then I'll go. I also have to wait until nobody's running up and down the roads looking for me, ready to string me up. That probably won't be until the dead of night, so I decide to stay put until then.

It's well into the afternoon; I can tell by the shifting light. I'm just about starving, so I sit on the floor of the granary, lean up against a bin and eat a bit of cheese on a chunk of bread. I savor it around in my mouth, it tastes so good. I haven't tasted cheese in nearly two years. Not since Tillie gave me some from her lunch pail at school. That was not long after I'd first come to the Brooks brothers' farm. For two months in the fall, I'd gone to school with ten other students. I never had any lunch, so I stayed away from the others when it was time to eat. I didn't want them to know I had no lunch. But my stomach was also so twisted with hunger that the smell of their food only made it worse.

On a day a few weeks into September, Tillie came to sit with me where I was perched on a rock by the creek.

I had a hard time looking at her. She was so pretty and soft-looking with her chestnut hair pinned up in curls, and her yellow dress flowing out from her hips. After smoothing her skirt beneath her, she sat next to me on the bank. She lifted a folded-up newspaper from her lunch pail and delicately began to unwrap it. Plunk in the middle of the paper sat a big slice of bread and cheese. I couldn't help but see it, sitting beside her the way I was. Tillie stopped what she was doing. I could feel her big eyes on me.

"Where's your lunch, Charlie?"

I pulled my eyes from the newspaper in her lap. I poked the stick I was fiddling with in the creek. "I already ate it."

"I didn't see you."

"I'm a fast eater." I finally got the gumption to look at her. "I'm sort of a magician that way, I guess."

This made her look at me strangely. I'd meant it to be funny, which, of course, it wasn't. She smiled a little anyway. "Well, you must have been very hungry to make it vanish that fast. Here, have mine too. I wish you would."

I hadn't eaten anything since the sour bowl of turnip soup Buck Brooks had given me the night before. I could have eaten that bread and cheese faster than any farm dog, but it was Tillie's lunch and she had to be hungry too. I shook my head.

"Charlie," she insisted, pushing the newspaper toward me, "I can't possibly eat it. I had a breakfast big enough for three. My oldest brother, Tom, moved to town to work at the bank, and my mother can't get out of the habit of cooking for him. Please, if you don't, it will only go to waste."

She now made like she'd never had any intention of eating it and that it was annoying her to have to hold it at all.

Not wanting it to go to waste, I began to think maybe I *should* take it. "You're sure?"

"Surer than I am that it'll snow before the winter's out. Here."

I accepted the newspaper and what was in it. As I ate, she continued to chat about what we were doing at school, pretending not to notice how I gobbled that bread and cheese.

After that, Tillie brought lunches big enough to feed the whole school. We'd sit by the creek, and now and again she'd sigh and tell me that her mother just couldn't keep in mind that she wasn't packing for Tom.

The barn door creaks, causing me to just about jump out of my britches. I haven't been paying attention— some fugitive-on-the-run I make. If I don't keep my wits about me, I'll be hung and stretched out on the table next to Albert before the day is out. I hop back into the oat bin, cover up and listen.

Whoever it is, they're treading very softly. They're so quiet going about their business that if I hadn't been listening intently, I wouldn't have heard them at all. The cows begin to low in their stalls directly across from the granary. It's not a bothered sound, but peaceful, like they're waiting for something that's part of their routine. A bit of wood scrapes against the floor. Soon I recognize the tinny sound of milk splattering into an empty pail. It has to be either Mrs. Carson or Tillie, come to milk the cows.

I peek around the door. Tillie is sitting on the milking stool with her back to me. She's speaking in a hushed voice. I don't want to scare the wits out of her, and I'm still not certain it's only her. I listen, but I don't hear anyone, so I dash quickly behind her, into the stall next to the one she's in.

"I'm sorry, Marigold," she is telling the cow she's milking. "I didn't mean to be so late. There's been a lot of commotion today and it couldn't be helped."

The cow I'm squatting beside suddenly decides to complain about me being there and hollers. I nearly die of a stopped heart myself.

"Dolores, I'm sorry to you too," Tillie tells her. "I'll be milking you right away. As I said, it's been a rather disastrous day. It seems Albert Brooks is dead, and they're looking all over for Charlie because Buck says he did it."

I can't listen any longer. "Tillie," I whisper. I don't want to talk too loudly because I'm still not one hundred percent certain she's alone.

Tillie keeps on milking.

"Tillie!"

Tillie jumps up, knocking the stool over. I peek above Dolores's back. Tillie's looking at Dolores like she's grown another head. Her eyes rise to me, standing above the cow, and her face darkens. Her hands fly to her hips. "Charlie! You just about scared me to death. I thought Dolores had got a voice."

"I'm sorry. But I couldn't exactly stand in the middle of the room to announce my presence."

Tillie's frown disappears as she wipes her hands on her apron. "Of course you couldn't. Charlie, where have you been? What happened?" Her skirt swooshes across the floor, sweeping up straw dust as she comes over to Dolores's stall and brushes oats from my hair.

"I've been hiding. Albert must have wandered out when I was sleeping and got turned around in the blizzard. I had nothing to do with it. When I found him he was already dead."

She nods. "Charlie, you know you're going to have to get out of here. Buck already has it in for you. You don't stand much chance against him."

"Yes," I tell her, "I'm aware. I just wanted you to know before I set out. I didn't want you to think I was the sort that would have done something like that."

Tillie throws her arms around me and pulls me close to her. It causes me to just about melt at the knees. "You didn't need to risk yourself to stay around and tell me that. I know it isn't in you to kill someone. I know how Albert and Buck treated you. Charlie, you should head west. To British Columbia. They're building the railroad and maybe you can get work."

I'm relieved. Tillie must believe me to be considering my situation. But she isn't able to continue. Her voice is drowned out by the sudden ruckus coming from the farmyard: a peal of sleigh bells, stamping horses, and men shouting orders and directions like they're running to the hounds. I rush to the crack in the wall. Tillie follows.

Mr. Carson and John have returned. With them are men from Macleod—officers from the North-West Mounted Police post, sitting tall astride their Irish thoroughbreds. They wear navy uniforms with shining brass buttons, and they carry revolvers at their sides. Buck bounces from the cutter.

"Let's spread out," he barks. His gaze then falls on the pitchfork John had left leaning against the woodpile. He grabs for it before whirling toward the barn.

"Buck!" One of the constables lays a hand on his arm. "I'm warning you again. We only want to talk to the lad. If you find him first, you bring him back here. No bloodshed, do you hear me? Or it'll be you that's going on trial."

Being told what to do only gets Buck madder. He elbows the officer before marching toward the barn.

"Quick!" Tillie grabs my hand. "Under the buggy." She pulls me toward the farm implements in a corner of the barn, but on the way I have a horrifying thought and break loose.

"My rucksack!" I tear back to the granary to collect my belongings. I'd left them on the floor by the oat bin. Nabbing them quick, I catch up with Tillie. She grabs my arm again and tugs me over to where an old horse buggy, the leather cracked and the wheels broken, sags against the wall. Tillie motions for me to crawl beneath it. "Get under it! Quick, Charlie! Don't come out until I come back after they're gone!"

It's a very tight fit, despite my being so thin-waisted. But I squish beneath it and pull my rucksack against my face. Tillie only has time to get away from the buggy before I hear the barn door get thrown open. I peek around my rucksack.

Tillie is picking up her milking stool and moving it over to Dolores's stall. With the force of a bull, Buck storms into the room past her.

"You seen that little coward come through here?" he roars.

"I beg your pardon?"

"Charlie Sutherland? You seen that skinny Home boy's hide? He's skulkin' around somewhere, but I'm going to get him. You seen him?"

"No, Mr. Brooks. I've just been milking Marigold and Dolores. I haven't seen Charlie in—well, must have been last summer when I was picking saskatoons down by the main trail."

Despite being scared to the bottom of my broken shoes, I smile inside. For someone so pretty, Tillie sure is a good liar. I would have never guessed it could be in her.

Buck ignores her. He begins rooting through the haymow, stabbing it with his pitchfork in a way that, if there were something living under there, it's not likely to emerge alive. Within a few minutes, Buck is joined by four or five of the Mounted Police. I can just see the door to the granary—two of them disappear into it. The rest spread throughout the barn.

Buck gives up on the haymow. He starts toward the horses' stalls, not ten feet away from me. I shrink against the wall beneath the buggy. He knocks something over. It falls, jolting the buggy. Burying my head behind my rucksack, I hold my breath.

∞

I remain scrunched beneath the buggy long after I hear the clatter of horses and cutters leaving the Carsons' farm. It's now evening, but I can't shake the picture of Buck standing silently over the buggy in the dark, just waiting to run me through with the pitchfork when I emerge. It's a fearsome enough image to keep me huddled where I am.

I may have drifted off awhile, I can't quite remember. It's Marigold and Dolores lowing softly that makes me jump. A light—a lantern, I determine, after peering around my rucksack—casts shadows like giant hawks soaring around the open barn. The light becomes brighter as it comes closer to the buggy.

"Charlie?"

It's Tillie's voice. I push aside the rucksack and crawl out. The smell of manure and sweaty animals rushes into my nostrils, but after being holed up all afternoon, it's a smell sweeter than lilacs blooming in May. I sit up and blink into the ring of lamplight. Marigold and Dolores loom in their stalls as dark ghosts behind the lantern's glow. Tillie sets the lantern on the floor. A sack hangs off her shoulder, and in her other hand, she holds something behind her pinafore.

"Charlie, are you alright? You must be just about starved. Here, I brought you some rabbit stew." She brings forth a bowl giving off such a delicious aroma I think I might faint. "Eat up. You'll like it."

She doesn't have to ask me more than once. I nod and, taking the bowl, try not to bolt it. Tillie also offers me a big slice of bread. Once she's satisfied that I'm eating, she swings the sack off her shoulder and sits next to me on the straw.

"You're going to have to get out of here tonight. Buck's rounding up a search party at the Macleod Hotel and coming back tomorrow. I've got some supplies together. If you head to British Columbia, you can get on logging or maybe fishing, and on the way you can work on the roads to get by. I overheard Father talking to John, and they're paying two dollars and fifty cents a day to the road crews. There's no stopping Buck. Father said he's got it in for you, even though no one else is convinced you bolted the cabin door and killed Albert Brooks. He's mean, Charlie. Buck doesn't have any kindness in him. He's spiteful and he's cruel."

All this has come out in a rush and Tillie is now staring at me, breathless. Her cheeks are rosy with the cold.

I've shoved enough food into my stomach so it isn't painful to stop eating. I smile at what she's said. "I know that about Buck."

Tillie's eyes drop to the lantern. "I'm sorry, of course you do." But just as suddenly they are flashing right back at me again. "Then you know what I'm saying is true."

After polishing off the stew, I set the bowl aside. I steady Tillie by the arms—I think her nerves are even worse than mine. "I've been thinking about it too. I'll start by heading into the mountains. There are the roads to work on, but there's also the railroad. Maybe I can get on with them."

Tillie motions toward the sack. "Father's old moccasin boots are in there. There's not much left of your shoes, and you're likely to lose your toes in this cold. I also packed in John's too-small mackinaw. Oh, and a new set of coveralls that belonged to Tom. He hasn't much use for them now that he's working at the bank. There's a little food, and a tin of matches and a skillet. And Charlie," Tillie pauses, like I'm not going to want to hear what she has to say next, "Buck's going to be passing it around. You're going to have to change your name."

I smile a little. "But I've got so fond of it. Drunken Alice gave it to me herself."

"Drunken Alice?"

The cabin door slams. "Tillie!" It's Mr. Carson's voice.

Tillie's voice drops to a hush. "Go on up to the hay-loft and wait. They're not going to be checking up there anymore tonight. You can start out in a couple of hours when everyone's sleeping."

We listen to the crunch of footsteps as her father approaches the barn. Tillie grabs the lantern and stands up. I don't know where my boldness comes from, but before she has a chance to turn for the door, I pull her to me. I think I'm just so pleased to have someone believe in me instead of thinking I'm low-down and no good. Tillie doesn't say anything. It just stops her a moment.

"Tillie!"

She gives me a little shove toward the ladder lead-ing to the hayloft. "Coming, Father." I scramble up the ladder as Tillie meets her father at the door. "I was just checking on Marigold and Dolores."

"Well, come on now. Mother's got your supper on."

I crawl beneath the eave in the hayloft, where I pull on Tom's new coveralls, the mackinaw and moccasin boots, and bury myself beneath the loose straw to stay warm. I picture Albert's frozen face. I then picture Buck's grizzled one. My heart takes a leap and I flinch despite the image of Buck only being in my mind. Once I recover, I realize I can no longer go back and work for him, even if the police say I'm innocent and even though I'm bound by the contract of Dr. Barnardo's Home. I haven't much of a plan about where I'm headed, and I don't know how I'll feed myself. But those mysteries aren't nearly so frightening as the thought of going back to live with Buck in that ramshackle cabin, all alone.

Three

It's a clear night when I start out with my rucksack fashioned from the rags of my bedclothes. A warm wind blowing in from the southwest whirls around me, and I can feel the temperature has already risen many degrees. A chinook is coming and by morning the snow will be melting from the fields, and the icicles hanging from the eaves will be dripping. I have to pass by the Brooks brothers' farm if I am to head west. But the moon is bright and the day's traffic of horses and men in their cutters hunting for me has packed down the snow, making it easy hiking along the trail.

As I near the farm, I see there is still a light in the cabin window. It casts a wash of yellow over the blue-tinged snow beneath. I stand at the edge of the property and look at the sorry mess of small sagging buildings. Many visitors have come by to visit Buck and, no doubt, express their sorrow for his troubles. The parade of animals has trampled the snow and turned the yard to muck. I'm not sure what prompts me to look inside, but I do. I creep to the window and peer above the ledge. The fire is going and the wick flickers in the lamp next to Buck's favorite willow chair. He isn't in it, though. He doesn't seem to be anywhere about the cabin. But there is Albert, laid out on the table, straight as the wooden slab itself. His hands lie clasped across his chest, and he is wearing a black suit I've never once seen on him.

A hinge wheezes behind me, making me jump. It belongs to the stable door. I dodge around the corner of the cabin, where I squat in the shadows and watch Buck emerge from the stable, a whiskey bottle dangling from one hand. He sniffs and rubs his nose as he walks unsteadily toward the cabin door. He stumbles on the stoop before disappearing inside. I sneak back to the window, where I watch him sit at the table and nestle a short glass between Albert's clasped hands. He fills it with whiskey. "A last drink together," he says, his halting voice carrying through the frosty windowpane. "Here's to you, brother." He clinks Albert's glass with the bottle, knocking the contents all over Albert's funeral suit, before taking a long swig from the bottle himself.

I suddenly feel sorry for Buck and his loss. Not that I particularly liked either him or Albert, not after the ill way they used me, but you don't need to like somebody to feel for their situation. Buck and Albert were kin to each other. It was the softest show of affection I'd ever seen from Buck.

I slip away from the window. I have one more thing to do—I have to say goodbye to the dapple grays. Duke and Duchess are happy to see me. I stand between them, stroking them, after feeding them a handful of turnips. I think how, after I leave, they'll go back to being just dumb animals. They won't hear their names anymore. Buck and Albert had never called them anything; it was me that had come up with their names. When I'd asked Albert what names they went by, he'd only bellowed, "Names? Them workhorses don't have names, Charlie Sutherland. It's foolish and sentimental to be naming dumb animals." But I had to call them something. I had to be able to address them when I praised them for being well-behaved.

I feed Duchess another chunk of turnip. The place isn't much to say goodbye to, but it's all I've known for coming up three years. So many times I'd planned to run off—usually after a good walloping from Buck. But I'd never been able to work up the nerve. I was stopped by the stories I'd heard at school of boys in my situation who'd tried to leave the homes they were sent to and froze to death. Or, in other ways, they died trying to escape. At least I was still alive at the Brookses, while those others were dead.

I say a few last words to Duke and, as quietly as I can, close the stable door.

I first came to live at the Brooks brothers' farm in June of 1900, sent to work on their homestead by Dr. Barnardo's Home. The Brookses had put in a request for a sturdy boy to help with the chores, in exchange for a place to live and eat. I wasn't half as thick as some, but I guess those making the decisions at the home figured I at least wouldn't get blown over in a prairie wind. Until I arrived in Winnipeg, I had never heard of a homestead or Macleod or the North-West Territories.

I was born near Watford, in the county of Hertford-shire, England. If I'm remembering it all correctly, I lived on a farm with my family until I was about five. As time comes between me and my childhood, I don't know anything about me for sure. Not even my name. The Charlie part I think is right. I don't recall ever being called anything different. But the Sutherland part is not so certain. The headmaster at Stepney Causeway told me that was the closest they could make out of what Drunken Alice wrote down when she brought me in.

"Miss Alice was obviously not too many years in school. Besides, Sutherland's as good a name as any," he assured me. "And anyway, Charlie, it's not the name a boy comes in with that's important. It's what he makes of what's inside."

I figure I was about six years old when I was first put in the receiving home at Stepney Causeway in East London. This was sometime after my father was crushed by the horse he was riding when it fell on him after tripping in a badger hole.

When my father died, he left my mother with seven children. The owner of the farm where my father had been a plowman had no reason to keep a poor woman and her whole brood. We moved from the cottage on the farm to London. My mother's sister, Lizzie, and her husband, Pius Monkley, took us in. Pius worked as a pointer in a needle mill, where he sharpened needles against a revolving grindstone thirteen hours a day. His face was a web of thin white scars caused by slivers of flying metal. My aunt and uncle had three children of their own.

Not long after the move, my mother was taken to a sanitorium suffering from consumption. I never saw her again. I don't expect she's still alive. I was never sent back to her, and as far as I know, she never tried to find me. So I figure she must have died.

Pius made a modest wage when we first came to live with them and nothing at all a few months later. He lost his position after coming down with pointer's rot from the stone and metal dust he inhaled all day. As the food in the house grew thinner, so did Pius's temper. At night, my brother Jack and I would lie in bed and hear him roar—Bugger and blast!—how was he to clothe and feed ten children? And why should he be expected to when he'd played no part in bringing seven of them into this world?

After one of these nights, Aunt Lizzie contacted someone. A woman came to the house, and, one by one, my sisters were taken away. One night, when it was only Jack and me left, he shook me awake.

"Charlie," he whispered, "it's time we struck out on our own. If we don't, they're going to pull us apart, and we won't ever see each other again. Get up and get your belongings. We'd best be out of here."

Jack was three, maybe four, years older than me, and it was a fearful thought to be separated from him. I quickly did what he said.

The next two nights we slept in a barrel beneath a railway arch. A few days later, the bit of cake and stump of black pudding we'd taken from Aunt Lizzie's was gone. We strolled the alleys, searching the gutters for rinds, begging people for so much as a crust. But there were many like us without homes and in need of food.

It was mid-morning and smoke from the early morning coal fires filled the air. Toward noon a pea-souper set in and I could barely make out my fingers at the end of my outstretched arm. I clung to Jack for fear of getting separated. I was so hungry, I couldn't stop the tears that set to rolling. Jack promised he would find me some bread.

"Climb in here and wait," he told me when we arrived back at the barrel.

Once again, I did what Jack said.

"I'll be back as soon as I can with something to eat." Jack looked up and down the alley. He was about to start out, but he seemed to think of something he needed to say. "Remember, Charlie, if anyone ever asks, you come from honest folk and your father was a farmer. A plowman who could draw the straightest furrows in the county. The leader of the plow team, he was."

Jack never came back. All day, I squatted in that barrel, listening to the sound of horses' hooves and wagons clacking over the stones in a light drizzle of rain, the bells and cries of the street pedlars and, closer to me, rats skittering across the pavement.

When it became very dark, I continued to wait. I lay there trying to pick out the glimmer of a star through the smoke and cloud. I could hear women laughing, spilling out of the gin parlors into the street. Men laughing too, in a deeper, stranger way. I kept thinking about what Jack had told me and wondering what my father looked like because I had no memory of him. I imagined he looked like Jack, only much bigger, with a black beard. I must have fallen asleep because the next thing I knew it was day and I was getting rained on. Large flakes of black ash from the chimney pots stuck to my face. I couldn't take the pain in my stomach, so I climbed out to find myself something to eat.

I'd been wandering down the wet cobblestones a good part of the day when a crooked hand, clutching a plum, thrust before me. My eyes followed the arm. It was attached to a wretched old woman. Dark veins stood out from her temples, and her skin and eyes were as yellow as the yolk of an egg. She horrified me and I jumped back. She pushed the plum closer, just beneath my nose. "Are you hungry, boy?"

My stomach tightened and saliva filled my mouth; I could already taste its fleshy, cold sweetness. There was no point lying. I nodded. I was afraid to take my eyes off her, but I couldn't take my eyes off that plum.

"I'll give you this. But there's a whole lot more where this came from. If you follow me."

That was how I came to live with "Drunken Alice." Her man, Ned Watts, was a hawker. He wasn't a drunkard like Alice, but he was a heartless and wicked man. He beat Alice and he used a birch switch on me. Ned sent me into the streets to sell matches. After one particularly bad caning for having my goods stolen, Alice must have taken pity on me. She snuck me out of the tin hut where we lived and took me to Barnardo's Home.

"Reason for admittance?" Mr. Wittecombe, a kind, clean-smelling man, asked Drunken Alice.

I stood next to her, clutching her dirty, patched-up skirt. Mr. Wittecombe's black shiny shoes caught my eye. I stared at them a moment before looking down at the rags tied around my own feet.

"He's an orphan," Drunken Alice said before fortifying herself with a pinch of snuff.

Mr. Wittecombe invited us into a room where I sat on the softest chair I'd set my bottom on in my entire life. He sat across from us at a wide desk with a plate of biscuits. He offered me the plate. I took three biscuits before Drunken Alice gave me a smack to tell me that was enough. She took a couple herself. But she didn't eat hers. She wrapped them in her filthy handkerchief, which she folded and tucked in her apron.

"No parents, then?"

"Not a one."

I looked at Alice briefly. Even as young as I was, I knew this wasn't quite true. But I was too interested in the place we were in and the biscuit I was chewing on to complain.

"Where'd you get the boy?"

"Found him on the street. He was beggin' for food. Followin' me. Wouldn't leave me alone, the little gnat."

"When was that?"

"More than a month ago. He's been livin' with me ever since. But Mr. Watts ain't too kindly toward him, so it's time we gave him up."

Mr. Wittecombe bent over a scribbler. He picked up his pen, dipped it in the inkstand and spoke aloud as he wrote. "Orphan boy. Nothing definitely known about his parentage. Father and mother believed to be dead. Child is clothed in rags." He glanced across at me, squinted, twisted his mouth and put his head down to write again. "And very dirty." When he was finished, he looked at Drunken Alice again. "Birthdate?"

Drunken Alice shook her head.

Mr. Wittecombe turned his eyes to me. "Charlie, do you know what day of the year you were born?"

"No, sir."

"Do you know how many years you are?"

Jack had once told me I was five, but that seemed like some time ago. "No, sir."

Mr. Wittecombe took one more long look at me before dipping his pen in the inkstand once more. "Date of birth, first of May 1886. Owing to the absence of any information about the child's birth, I am allocating this date as being about right." Mr. Wittecombe made a flourish with the end of his pen, stuck it in the inkstand, stood up and offered me his hand. "Welcome to your new home, Charlie."

My small hand was wet from sucking the cookie flavor from it. I put it in Mr. Wittecombe's massive one.

I was treated decently at Stepney Causeway, Dr. Barnardo's large orphanage in London. I had a bed in a dormitory where all the strays and orphans slept. But I was only there a few months before I was sent to my first foster home.

I was given to the care of the Matleys in Whitechapel. They were kind enough, but they already had four children, and I wasn't sure why they wanted another. There was already not enough to go around and they were always squabbling among themselves. After a year or so, it must have occurred to them that I *was* more than they could handle. I was sent back to Stepney. There were three more foster homes after that.

According to the birthdate assigned to me by Mr. Wittecombe, I was nearly thirteen when I arrived home from the national school to see an unfamiliar horse and buggy outside my foster home. Inside the house waited a man from the orphanage I had never met. He told me I'd been selected to go to Canada. I was returned to Stepney Causeway, where I was given medical and intelligence examinations. I must have passed because in April of that year I boarded the S.S. Sicilian and set out from Liverpool along with other boys who were on their way to farms in Canada. They looked every bit as frightened as I felt.

We left the dock and the coastline faded until we were surrounded by nothing but gloomy, gray sea. We were ten days on the water. Each morning we were awakened by the sharp command, "All out!" I'd roll from my berth and join the line of boys scuffling toward the washhouse. We ate breakfast—rows and rows of us—at long wooden tables in the great hold below.

At night I was kept awake by a dull vibration beneath my berth. As we got farther out, the swells became larger and the ship began rolling. Many of us, including me, became violently sick. Our long hours were then spent struggling with the seasickness and the nurses who were convinced a good brisk march around the deck was the cure. Toward the end of our voyage we sailed through fields of icebergs. For the most part they passed silently, but if we were standing on deck and they drifted close enough, the roar of shifting ice echoed through the air like gunfire. I worried that we might run into one at night. "Won't ever happen," a ship hand assured me. "Us experienced sailors can smell icebergs from miles away." I wasn't much convinced—I could smell nothing beyond the coal fires driving the ship. We slowed considerably around the Newfoundland Banks, where the foghorn blew every few minutes. We sailed the St. Lawrence River at night and docked in Point Levis, Quebec.

Here we each received a trunk containing our Canadian Outfit. Along with the jumpers, nightshirts and other items of clothing, each trunk contained a hymn book, a *Traveler's Guide* and a copy of *The Pilgrim's Progress*. This last book I have read many times since. It was written by Mr. John Bunyan and it's about a chap named Christian who sets out from the City of Destruction after he learns it will be destroyed by fire. He heads for a place called the Celestial City. Mr. Bunyan writes about the good and bad circumstances Christian runs into along the way. He tells about the folks who help him, like Evangelist. And he tells about the nasty ones, like Mr. Worldly Wiseman, who doesn't appear to be nasty, but as Christian finds out, it's all a trick. Then there are the downright evil folks that try to prevent Christian from continuing on his journey. One of these is Apollyon, who has scales like a fish and breathes fire. He throws a flaming dart at Christian's breast.

Once we boarded the Grand Trunk Railway, I said goodbye to my mates from the boat. I knew I wasn't likely to ever see them again. We were all going some place different. I traveled farther than most. The train crossed southern Quebec, and while many got off at stops in Ontario, I stayed on to Winnipeg. I had been at the Winnipeg Distributing Home for a month when the Brooks brothers' request came in.

I sat on the edge of a hard seat in a coach waiting to leave the Winnipeg train station. The engine wheezed like a sleeping dragon, now and again releasing a puff of steam. Finally we set out, hissing, clacking and squealing; belching smoke into a clear blue sky. I was terrified, but my stomach was also tied up with excitement. I was finally getting close to my new home. We traveled across the Districts of Assiniboia and Alberta. For most of the journey, I sat up in the coach; I couldn't sleep for the knot in my stomach, but also because I had never seen land so stark and flat. We passed lakes, the train platforms of many small settlements and the giant skulls and rib cages of thousands of slaughtered buffalo, their white bones scattered, gleaming in the dust. One afternoon, mountains appeared far to the west. It had been flat for so long I wondered if I was seeing things.

That evening, the train pulled into the station at Macleod. It was there, on the station platform, that I first set eyes on Albert Brooks.

The Canadian Pacific was long gone, and I'd been sitting on my trunk on the platform for coming up two hours before Albert showed. I had worked myself into a terrible state of nerves by then. All kinds of things had been going through my mind. I wondered if the conductor had told me the wrong place to jump off, or if the Brooks brothers had decided they didn't want me and hadn't bothered to tell the home. I had no money and no one to contact. I hadn't even considered what to do if no one appeared. Three times I questioned the stationmaster, but he seemed unconcerned. Each time he reassured me my new employer would be along. "He won't forget you. It wouldn't be like Albert to pass up a free hand. Particularly with summer coming and so much work to be done."

I should have clued in right then and there.

"Charlie Sutherland!"

The tone wasn't so pleasant, but I was relieved that somebody seemed to know my name. I turned. Albert Brooks sat high on his wagon seat, holding tight to his horses' reins. He wore a worn, tweed shirt with red braces, brown britches and a beat-up felt hat. His peppery-gray hair and whiskers were massed together beneath it, and before I'd thought to respond, I thought how much he looked like a sheep before it is shorn.

"Well, if you want what's yours, you'd best get off it and haul it over here. It's not goin' to walk over by itself."

I sat and stared a minute longer, trying to get my bearings. At least Albert Brooks had known what to expect, and he could see it right in front of him: a scrawny English boy looking like he didn't belong. But he and his gruff talk and gruffer appearance were altogether a surprise to me.

"Charlie Sutherland, I ain't got time to waste waitin' for you to watch the sun set. Boy, come on and get over here. If you don't, I won't be leavin' just your trunk behind, but you along with it."

Immediately, I jumped off the trunk and dragged it across the platform to the dirt road. I struggled to get it into the horse cart while Albert sat there, chewing a wad of tobacco, watching me. Finally realizing I couldn't manage on my own, he clambered off the cart and, without a word, lifted an end. Once I was sitting next to him, he spat the wad into the dirt and loosened the reins.

The horses—a couple of gray shires—trotted ahead. Over the course of the ten-mile ride north to the homestead on Willow Creek, I observed that they did everything exactly as Albert Brooks said. I decided right then and there that those horses probably knew best, and, considering the rough nature of the man who sat next to me, I'd be wise to do the same.

The trail was the worst I'd ever been on, made treacherous with ridges, depressions and great clods of earth where carts had become stuck when water poured through the ruts. But Albert seemed to know the trail well and steered his horses away from the hazardous parts.

Nothing had prepared me for the sight of their ramshackle cabin, squatting off the side of the wagon trail, poorly chinked with clay and straw. I was soon to discover that the roof of shingles and building paper allowed snow to fly in my face in winter, and it leaked in the spring and summer when it rained. Months later, I figured they stuck me in the loft to keep something warm between them and the weather because the roof did little good. In the three years since they'd come out from Ontario, they'd also managed to build themselves a pig shed, a sod chicken house, an icehouse and a small barn.

When I first came across Buck Brooks, pumping water in the barnyard, he struck me to be as rough and as hardened as his brother. He was the younger one by about five years.

"Well, so this is Charlie Sutherland," he said, squinting up at me as Albert reined in the horses. "How be you jump down here, boy, and carry these buckets in to fill the pig troughs. And when you've done that, you can shovel the manure out of their pens. The cart to fill is next to the stable over there."

The buggy hadn't even come to a stop and I'd already been given a list of chores.

I started in and I didn't stop until long after midnight. It's most unpleasant to think how many tons of pig, cow, horse and chicken manure I've shoveled into that same cart since then.

Four

I strike out along the trail going west, with all that I own over my shoulder. I'm glad for the mackinaw and the moccasins Tillie has given me. My feet have never been so warm in all the miles I've put on them since coming to the farm. But my mind is not so comfortable. After a while it seems to be wearing out. It begins playing tricks on me, taking advantage of my being full of fear and tuckered out.

A sound behind me makes me stop and turn more than once. After walking and listening closely for the next few steps, I realize it's only the echo of my own feet on the crisp snow. An owl swoops out of the black sky. It passes close to my face with a low *whoosh*, giving me an awful start. Phantom cattle, hidden in the darkness, snuffle against a fence, and all the while the coyotes never stop wailing. A lone coyote strikes up—perhaps warning another of my presence. An entire pack of them winds up to a full chorus of yowling and caterwauling, then trails off, only to start over again.

I stop to catch my breath. I figure I should try to keep going at least until daylight, when I can find a place to hole up. I'll sleep during the day when Buck will be looking for me. I'll be able to think better after that.

The trail on either side is broken only by a smattering of farms. A band of cloud has moved in with the wind, and although I can smell wood smoke, I often can't make out the buildings until they are right in front of me.

I've been walking maybe two hours and have just passed another cabin when a figure lurches across the trail in front of me. It's roughly the shape of a human, but it's huge, as tall as a ship's mast, and it lopes like an animal, a black bear or a timber wolf. A thought stops me right where I am. It's a wetigo. Tillie had described them one day as we were eating lunch.

"Big hairy creatures that live in the woods," she'd told me. "The Indians believe they eat only human flesh. They have a taste for it. Sometimes their spirit enters into a person and that person becomes like them. It's happened. My mother's told me stories of whole families that were eaten after someone in the family turned into one."

I can't force myself to go any farther. I'm certain that whatever it is, it's waiting in the culvert on the other side of the trail ahead. I glance quickly behind me to see how far back the last cabin was. I turn forward again. I don't see it. But that isn't surprising because as Tillie had gone on to say, after leaning in close to make her point, "A wetigo is known to be so skinny that when it faces you from the front, it disappears. It could be creeping right toward you and you wouldn't even see it."

And suddenly—there it is! The figure rises from the culvert and, backed by moonlight, begins moving swiftly toward me, monstrous and hairy, with long arms swinging, working back and forth like pistons. I turn and hightail it toward the last cabin I'd passed.

I plunge through snowdrifts higher than my moccasins, but my fear makes me spring right up again like a frightened jackrabbit. Guided by moonlight, I head for a shed next to the last cabin. Ten feet in front of it, the wetigo throws its heavy arms around me and I fall flat on my face with it on top of my back.

"I'm starving," it snarls in a raspy voice. "I've got to have something to eat."

I struggle hard. I try to scramble up and throw it off, but it's pinning me down, kneeling on the low part of my back. Its breath is horribly rancid.

"Please," I beg in a desperate voice and in a most pitiful way—I've had a lot of experience with pitiful characters in my life, and I can be most convincing when called upon. "I'm not much of a meal, sir. I haven't had a decent one myself in my entire life. I wouldn't be much nourishment to you."

But instead of chomping into me, the wetigo climbs off my back. "What are you talking about, boy?"

With the weight gone, I flip over. I squint up at a gnarled old man. A tuft of hair sprouts from his chin, as ragged as an old buffalo's beard. He wears a tattered sheepskin hat. His face is awfully thin and his cheeks are dark depressions.

"I'm about starved," he repeats. "I haven't eaten a morsel in two days. Don't you have anything in that pack of yours a hungry fellow could munch on?"

I am so relieved to see a regular man in front of me, I fall back with a little laugh.

"What's so funny, boy? Are you plumb crazy? Is that why you're running around on your own in the dead of winter in the middle of the night? Let me look in there."

I sit up. But before he can wrench the sack from my shoulder, I take it off and toss it to him. "I've got some bread and cheese, and there's some tinned meat in there. Help yourself. You can have whatever you want. But I'm going into the shed to warm up."

He roots through my rucksack as he follows me into what turns out to be a granary. He's tearing into the bread before we've even passed through the door. I sit on the floor and lean against a wall. A bit of moonlight falls from the one window over my head. I'm breathing heavily from both the effort of running and the fear that started me off.

The old man sits across from me. He holds what he's eating awkwardly, seeming to need both hands to get it into his mouth. I look a little closer in the thin light. His hands, or at least what's left of them, are bound in tattered and dirty strips of gunny sacking. I can't detect any fingers on them. He sees me studying them.

"I lost my fingers in a railroad accident when I was laying track. My hands got crushed beneath a pile of ties that tumbled when we were moving them." As he speaks, he doesn't slow down eating but tears off another chunk of bread with his teeth. The food churns in his mouth. "There's no job for a man with no hands when it comes to building a railroad, and they wouldn't take me back. That was two years ago. I've been living by my wits ever since."

The old man stops chewing long enough to grin and extend his left hand toward me. "Name's Cyrus Jones. But those who know me call me Fingers. That's on account of these." Cyrus holds up a full index finger and the stub of his littlest one. "I only got two fingers, well, technically one and a half. But I'm practiced at using them so fast they say I work like a man who owns twenty."

I'm not quite sure how to shake the hand of a man with only one and a half fingers. I do so most carefully. "Pleased to meet you, Cyrus Jones. I'm Charlie—"

I suddenly remember what Tillie had said. I can't use my name with Buck searching for me. I think as quick as I can, and instead I come up with Mr. Wittecombe's name—the man from Stepney Causeway with the plate of biscuits on his desk.

"Wittecombe—Charlie Wittecombe."

"Well, Charlie, it's a real pleasure to meet you and I thank you for the meal. Now, I've told you what I'm doing out here in the middle of the night. What about yourself? By the manner of your words, I'd guess you to be a Home boy. And the fact that I run into you traveling down the road in the dead of night, carrying what you own over your shoulder, I'm only guessing, but I'd say you're running away from something. Would that be about right?"

I don't say anything right away. I don't want to incriminate myself, but there obviously isn't any fooling Cyrus Jones, who gets by on his wits alone. "Yes, sir, you are right on both accounts."

Cyrus keeps his eye on me as he gobbles down a tin of beef, scooping it out with the buck knife he'd found in my pack. It's an awkward sight to take in, watching him operate that knife with his one-and-a-half fingers. I'm a little suspicious that if it slips—and the way he's clumsily wielding it makes that seem very possible—he might lose the couple of fingers he has left. In my opinion, he certainly doesn't look as adept with them as he's made himself out to be, or as the nickname that others have given him would suggest.

"What are you running from, Charlie Wittecombe?"

Again, there seems no sense in falsifying my answer when he seems the type who will discover the truth no matter what. "It's the result of a misunderstanding. The fellow I work for thinks I'm responsible for the murder of his brother." I then tell Cyrus my story of finding Albert frozen, with a whiskey bottle clutched in his hand.

When I finish, Cyrus is thoughtful for a minute. "And where are you off to now?"

"I'm heading west. I'm looking for work where I can get it."

Cyrus sets the empty beef can aside. He leans forward. "Young lad, it sounds like your run of luck is about as favorable as mine. I'll tell you what. Why don't you and me team up for a while? About five miles back I passed an establishment advertising for ice cutters. Fifty cents a day. We could sleep here tonight, then go back tomorrow and get us some work for a few days. We'll work better together, and I can look out for you. You've got a full set of fingers, and I can handle any curious questions and answer them to your benefit. I mean, considering you're running from the law and all. And once we have some money in our pockets, you can go west like you plan, and I can head back to my family in the East."

I consider what he's said. I can't find any hitches in his plan. As it is, I don't have a penny, and I'm not likely to be noticed as readily if I'm in the company of someone else. Not like I will be if I'm traveling on my own. "Alright," I agree. "That sounds reasonable enough."

Cyrus nods, stands up, stretches and begins sweeping the loose straw into a pile with his foot. "Well, Charlie, that meal about wore me out. I'm going to turn in now, and I suggest you do the same. Tomorrow we'll go to work."

The fingerless old man lies down on his pile of straw, sighs contentedly, and within minutes he's snoring as loudly as Albert Brooks once did.

With the first crow of the rooster, Cyrus and I set out for the farm that's advertising for ice cutters. We'll be working for Mr. Appleton, who sells ice to others at four dollars a ton. The terms are fifty cents a day, plus one meal and a small bunkhouse to sleep in. After being supplied with ice saws, axes, hooks, hatchets and a team of oxen to haul the ice cakes back to the icehouse, we're directed a mile along a trail to Ritchie's Pond.

It's warmed up considerably with the chinook that has blown in during the night. The surface of the ice has a skim of melted snow on it, making it especially slippery to work. We have to watch that we don't slide into the open water where we've already cut. Using the long blade, I score and saw the ice we're harvesting into slabs. Cyrus guides the slabs toward us with the long-handled hook. After a while, he complains that he's losing his grip. He hands me the tool, stands aside and watches. It's a struggle to get the slabs hauled out of the water and onto the ice where we're working, particularly with Cyrus not having any fingers to speak of. Once I manage the first few, I begin cutting the slabs into smaller cakes. I split them with the hatchet—something else Cyrus can't wield.

As the morning rolls along, Cyrus removes himself from the ice cutting. He sits back on the stoneboat where he chews tobacco and watches me work. Now and again he squirts a fountain of juice from his mouth, leaving a brown hole in the snow, before giving me a lecture on how to improve my work. He suggests that I should change the angle of the hatchet when striking it. He tells me that if I was smart, I'd use the handle of the hook as a lever to aid in lifting the blocks. His lessons never include actually getting up and pitching in. I realize he's held back by his injury, but I sure begin to doubt that he's earned his nickname Fingers because he's a man who likes to work.

Once the stoneboat's loaded, Cyrus drives the team to the icehouse, a mile back by the main house. I unload the cakes of ice, and after lowering them into the pit, I cover them with sawdust. We make three trips between Ritchie's Pond and the icehouse; me cutting, chopping and hauling, and Cyrus directing, supplying tips on improving my work and napping on the stoneboat while I fill it up. We quit when it's too dark to work. About seven o'clock, Mr. Appleton brings a crock of partridge stew and biscuits into the bunkhouse. He thanks us for our work, saying that he is pleased with our efforts and accomplishments.

Cyrus Jones steps forward. "Why, thank you, sir," he says with a little bow. "I aim to work hard and not let up for a respectful employer like yourself. I try to be an example for the boy, here, who hasn't had much exposure to honest work."

I look over at Cyrus, standing there all puffed up like an excited bird. How does he know what I've been "exposed to"? And it seems to me he's done nothing but "let up" all day.

Mr. Appleton pays us our fifty cents—two shinplasters each. He invites us to stay and cut ice for a couple more days if we can.

I'm still not used to eating until my stomach is full up, particularly a meal so tasty. By the time I realize I'm about ready to burst, I'm also ready to fall asleep. I hoist myself onto the top of one of the three sets of bunks. As I'm lying there with my stomach full, I think how for the first time since I've come to Canada, I have fifty cents of my own tucked into my rucksack. Cyrus Jones is turning out to be something of an idler, but I'm grateful to work for Mr. Appleton, who appears appreciative of my work.

Two more ice cutters sign up with Mr. Appleton after daybreak. Danny and Donald McKay are cousins who are not much more than twenty years old and are looking to make money in order to buy supplies. They both live on homesteads with their parents and younger brothers and sisters east of Red Deer Crossing. They're of Scottish descent—originally from a village called Dechmont.

Cyrus removes himself even further from working now that we have two extra pairs of hands. He spends most of the day lazing on the stoneboat, directing the three of us: me, Danny and Donald. The only time he makes a show of working is when Mr. Appleton comes around to check on our progress. Then he makes out like it was his idea to organize us with me cutting, Danny raking in the ice cakes, and Donald splitting and piling them to be hauled—when actually it was Donald who'd come up with the plan.

The McKays have patience, though, and they don't complain about Cyrus Jones. They're happy fellows, who take him as a crippled man and ignore his lazy ways. Unlike me. After two days of him, I have to hold back on lifting a foot to trip him so he falls headfirst into the pond.

The three of us work well together. We make six trips between Ritchie's Pond and the icehouse that first day. Mr. Appleton pays us, and we sit about the bunkhouse in the evening after another good meal. Danny and Donald each light a pipe. Cyrus laments that he had his own tobacco pipe stolen when employed as a navvy with the railroad. Donald is kindly, and when he hears this, he offers his own to Cyrus Jones.

Donald then lies back on his mattress, clasps his big hands behind his head and lets a last smoke ring drift off toward the rafters. "Tell me, Charlie, once you get a real job and make yourself some money, what do you have in mind to do?"

It's a question I haven't taken the time to consider. When I left the Carsons, all that was really on my mind was putting distance between me and Buck. "I haven't given it much thought. For now, I'm headed west in search of work where I can get it."

"Well, I'll tell you, what you want to do is eventually buy yourself some land. The government's offering a quarter section at a cost of ten dollars to anyone who has it in them to farm it. Now, that's what I'm going to do in a year or two. Once my dad gets settled and can manage on his own. You're somebody when you've got your own place."

Of course I'd seen the advertisements, but I'd never imagined it could apply to me. Not considering the humble circumstances I was living in, or those that I came from. I begin thinking about me on my own land, plowing and sowing my own fields. On a place of my own I could manage things the way I saw fit, and nobody could take it away from me.

"What specifically does a fellow have to do to get this land?"

"Like I said, you've got to break sod and farm it, prove you can do it in the space of three years. All the advertisements say is you've got to be eighteen and able-bodied. You're headed west. You should try and get on at one of the mines in the Crow's Nest Pass. I hear they pay as much as three dollars a day. With those kind of wages it wouldn't be long before you could afford it. That's where we plan to work once our dads are on their feet."

I now think seriously about what having my own place would be like. I'll have to wait until I'm eighteen to apply, but that gives me more than a year to make some money. I begin adding things up to see how much I'll need. There will be the ten dollars for the land. I'll need a team of horses to clear it and for transportation—that will run me around about two hundred dollars for a reliable one. Harnesses cost another thirty. I'll need a riding plow, or I could get by with a walking one. That will be twenty dollars or so more. I'll have to buy seed, a cow and some chickens, but I'll eventually grow my own feed for the animals.

"You could have your own place, like those brothers Brooks," Cyrus Jones interrupts my calculations. "And you wouldn't ever have to work for the likes of them again."

"Who are the brothers Brooks?" Donald unhitches his braces.

Before I can shush him, Cyrus tells him, and it sure isn't to my benefit, like he'd promised he would answer any curious questions if asked.

"They was who Charlie Wittecombe was working

for before he ran away. He's accused of murdering one of them."

I am so surprised he's laid it all out in the open with nobody wrestling it out of him, I sit with my mouth agape. I must look as dumb as the ox that hauls the stoneboat. I can't see how it could possibly be helpful to him to let others in on my predicament. It seems to me that since we arrived together, he only risks being let go on my account. But whatever his reason for telling them, Donald and Danny McKay are now scrutinizing me in a most uncomfortable way. I know as sure as I want to lunge forward and strangle Cyrus Jones that they are searching for the murderer in me.

Since Cyrus obviously has no intention of jumping in to my defense, I do it for myself. "It was all a misunderstanding." And as quick as I can, with my words tumbling into one another, I explain about Albert's death.

After listening to what I have to say, to my relief, the McKays agree that it does sound like an accident. They then announce they're ready to turn in for the night.

We cut ice for two more days following Cyrus Jones's announcement that I'm a runaway murderer. I'm not certain, but I detect a little hesitation in the friendliness of the McKays after the conversation that night. There isn't much point in saying anything to Cyrus Jones about it. He most certainly isn't turning out to be the hard-working, helpful chap he had professed to be.

I have two dollars in my rucksack, and the McKays each have one dollar and fifty cents, when I lie down to sleep after my fourth day of work.

Five

I don't sleep as soundly as I have on the first few nights. I have too many concerns about my future running through my head. The bunkhouse is also a noisy place, with all the snoring and coughing and spluttering. Being uneasy of mind anyway, those noises grate on my nerves like there's a steam engine braking in my head. But finally I do doze off.

The sky is black as pitch and the moon is shining bright when I snap awake again. Someone is slinking around the foot of my bed. I can't see clearly, but by his movements—lifting and setting things aside—he seems to be looking for something. The silhouette of his head in the moonlight tells me it's Cyrus Jones.

"Cyrus?"

He stiffens before lowering what's in his hands. "Charlie, I'm just making a run for the outhouse. Go back to sleep." The door opens and Cyrus Jones leaves. I fall asleep again.

It's Cyrus crowing at the top of his scrawny lungs that

wakes me the next morning. He lets out a holler from where he stands between the bunks.

"I been robbed!" he bellows louder than a foghorn on a ship, causing me and the McKays to jump from our sleep. "Robbed o' my wages for the last few days. Which one of you layabouts is a thief?!"

Danny and Donald are immediately out of their bunks and trying to calm him. Cyrus pulls his empty pockets from his trousers—two dirty, empty cotton triangles hanging from his hips. "Not a penny to show for all the hard work I done. What kind of low-down scoundrel would rob what was owed an old man?" His eyes skim the three of us in the bunkhouse, twice over. Eventually, of course, they settle on me. He thrusts his left arm toward me, wagging his one whole finger inches from my face. "A Home boy. That's who'd rob an injured old man without a defense. A mangy street urchin who's used to scrabblin' and stealin' and don't think twice about it, that's who. Boys, I suggest you check your own earnings."

At Cyrus's suggestion, Donald lifts a stocking from his pack, where he must have stored his stash of money. He reaches into the toe to discover it's gone. Danny roots through a bundled handkerchief. He also finds his money missing. They all three turn to me.

Danny addresses me in a most unkindly way. "Why, you filthy little thief! What'd you take us for—thinking we were so stupid you could just rob us blind?"

"Cyrus," I say helplessly, "you know I don't have it in me. What are you trying to tell the McKays?"

"Don't have it in you!" Donald repeats, close to my face. "Didn't we just learn a few days ago you're accused of murder? I'd say you have it in you as much as Jesse James."

Cyrus marches to the end of his bunk, where he picks up the ice hatchet that's leaning against the wall. He turns back to me. "A kind old fellow like me takes the likes of you under his wing and gets paid back by being taken advantage of. Sit down," he says, pointing to my own bunk with the handle of the axe. "On your bunk there, boy." Once I do, Cyrus makes a show of sitting on a chair across the room, positioning it so it blocks the door. He lays the axe across his knees. "McKays, why don't you go get our employer and let him know what a common criminal he's hired. I'll wait here and guard the boy."

The McKays are hesitant to leave us alone. Danny questions Cyrus on how he'll manage if I jump him. "I mean, seeing as you're incapacitated with missing fingers," he gently explains.

"I have no intention of jumping him," I firmly tell him.

Danny gives me a nasty look to tell me he isn't speaking to me.

"I don't believe he will," Cyrus says. "There's too many of us about. It's not like he's all alone with me, as he was with that fellow he's accused of murdering."

After assuring themselves there are no other weapons near at hand, the McKays agree and head for Mr. Appleton's house.

"Why are you doing this?" I ask Cyrus as soon as I hear their footsteps receding toward the farmhouse.

With the McKays gone, Cyrus Jones quits performing and turns more into himself. "I didn't really want to, Charlie, but I have to take my opportunities where they present themselves. For a fellow with no fingers, finding money can be a bit of a chore. I was able to get some cash and now I'm ready to move on." From the folds of his clothes he brings forth a small sack. He shakes it. It jangles with coins. "You see, being who you are and the circumstances you come from, you're just particularly easy to blame. And I knew the McKay cousins would be quick to accept you were the thieving kind. So now I got to leave, now that my money bag is full. But I'll tell you what, I'll give you a head start if you want to take off now. They're going to be after you full force once Mr. Appleton discovers his jar of silver is empty too."

I shake my head. "Well, Cyrus Jones, that's mighty kind of you."

"The way things are sitting, it's the best I can do. You go ahead and strike out now. I'll wait until I see them coming back before I start hollering. I'll tell them you overpowered me." He makes a pretense of clutching his fingerless hands about his neck. He laughs. "Being the beast that you are."

I know Cyrus is leaving me no choice. Grabbing my rucksack, I head for the door.

"Oh, and Charlie? You'll want to keep low for a while. And another thing—it might be wise to use a different name."

I'm a good ways down the trail, ready to duck into the woods at any moment, when I hear Cyrus chirping, "That no-good Home boy—he struck out and got away!"

∞

After cutting off the trail into the bush, I plod through snow that's drifted knee-deep. I sprint across the bald, open spots where it's blown clear. Once I meet up with the railroad track, I follow it—it's easier than hiking through heavy snow.

After running full out for nearly an hour, I stop to catch my breath. The voices of the McKays had faded sometime before—they were driving horses and cutters and would have been forced to keep to the main trail.

A column of smoke wafts into the sky a mile or so in the distance. Another small building lies straight ahead. I shield my eyes to protect them from the glare of the bright sun on the white fields. There's no smoke, which makes me think it's to store grain and will be safe to hide out in until I can gather my thoughts and decide what to do next.

My eyes are full of reflected sunlight as I near the building. I blink. It's a railroad shed. The door is unlocked. Inside is a handcar of the type railroad workers use for inspecting the tracks. I have no intention of stealing it, but I can see no harm in borrowing it for an hour or two. It isn't in use, so it won't likely cause an inconvenience. And when I'm done, I'll leave it parked so it can easily be found on a sidetrack. It sure will be useful in putting some distance between me and the McKays and Buck Brooks.

I walk once around the handcar, inspecting what kind of vehicle I'm about to drive. After climbing on the platform, I release the brake and slowly work the pump handle up and down. The car creaks and groans like a metal giant waking, complaining at having to move out of the shed. But once the gears and grease warm up, I get it started along the rails that meet up with the main track.

A few more good pumps and it isn't long before I'm whirring along the track, making my way across fields that would take me hours to cover on foot. I gain speed and I'm soon flying past the homestead I'd spotted not fifteen minutes earlier. The track ahead appears clear and good.

I soon have a rhythm to my strokes. I pick up speed going down the long slopes, although I have to pump with all I have to make it up the rises now that the land is beginning to swell. I'm within sight of the foothills of the Rocky Mountains.

It's desolate country. I've passed only a few lonely homesteads in the space of a couple of hours when I realize my stomach is complaining again. After coming to a stop on a level stretch, I open my rucksack and, blimey!—if that Cyrus Jones hasn't gone and consumed every morsel of food I had. I check my stocking where I'd stored my own wages for cutting ice. The low-down thief has cleaned me out of my money too! I'm not sure why I thought he would have been kind enough to spare me when he'd pilfered the McKays' wages as well as Mr. Appleton's silver. I guess I'd just considered it was humiliation enough to be blamed for the thefts. Well, there's nothing to do but continue along and hope I'll find work of some sort ahead. I begin working the pump handle.

Once I'm soaring along again, I don't think much about how fun it is anymore. I can't enjoy it with the knowledge of what Cyrus has done seething away inside me. But the land is now flat and open, so I race along for a few more uneventful hours.

I'm shooting across the open plain when I glance down into a coulee. When I look up again, ten feet in front of me, where the north wind has cleared a passage across the prairie, is a drift nearly six feet high. Immediately throwing on the brake, I attempt a screeching, squealing stop. Despite my efforts, I plow into it. I'm thankful not a soul is around to witness my performance, because it would be awfully embarrassing. After scooping snow from my eyes and rubbing my cold, bruised nose, I step off the handcar. I follow the drift fifteen or so feet down the length of the track. Having nothing to shovel it with, I have no choice but to set out on foot again.

For most of the afternoon, I follow animal trails; the tracks lead across the open prairie, along the ridge of the coulee and eventually down into a shallow valley. It's easier walking where there are trees and the snow hasn't had the opportunity to drift. The smell of wood smoke becomes stronger, and I note areas where footprints left by treaded boots mingle with those of deer, coyote and elk. I'm nearing a settlement of some type. I work my way up to the open plain again.

I've walked another two or three hours when dark begins to settle in. I am tuckered out and in need of a warm spot to sit for a while. Thirty minutes later I come upon a schoolhouse. If I can just shut my eyes and think, even for an hour, I'll be refreshed and ready to go on again. I can see no harm in going inside and getting out of the wind and cold. I open the door. The room smells of dust, camphor oil and books. The stove in the center of the room still holds a little warmth, so I plunk myself in the desk closest to it, lay my head in my arms and close my eyes to catch my breath.

I must have fallen asleep because when I next open my eyes, I am greeted by the first grays of an early morning winter sky. The squeal of a door hinge echoes in my brain, and I realize this must have been what woke me. Footsteps sound in the mudroom.

"What's this, then? Do I spy a boy so anxious to get to school he sleeps in the schoolhouse so as not to be late?"

I sit up. A man of about sixty fills most of the doorway. His quiet blue eyes flicker in a face that, even after the long winter, is sunburned from decades spent outside. After saying this, he walks into the room and reaches for the wood bucket next to the stove. "Be another hour or so before anyone else turns up."

I nod, but I remain in the desk, where I am still trying to get my bearings.

He looks closer at me and frowns. "But I don't believe you go to this here Fishburne School. What's your name, son?"

"John…" I try to think quick for a second name. I catch a glimpse of a name written on the chalkboard at the front of the room. "Laurier, sir."

"John Laurier. Last name same as our prime minister's. That's a right French-sounding name for a Home boy, which I detect in your voice. Well, John Laurier, I'm Hector Barnes and I take care of this here little school-house. I don't recognize you as being from around here. Where do you come from, and where are you on your way to?"

I stand up, shuffling some to give me a few more seconds to think. It's an awful strain to have to do so much quick thinking when I'm feeling so dead on my feet. "I just left the home where I was living for the last few years. I'm of age and done there now. I'm headed out to the West Coast to find work."

Mr. Barnes nods, but he is again looking at me kind of quizzically. I'm sure he is wondering why I am so wispy if I'm of age. "Got something lined up there, have you?"

I shake my head that I don't. Mr. Barnes continues to study me. I can see he is trying to make out what sort of boy is standing in front of him.

"Those are some fine overalls you're clothed in. You must have come from a prosperous home. Decked you all out before you left, did they?"

"Yes," I say, suddenly uncomfortable in Tom's too-big overalls, "they did."

Mr. Barnes nods. "Most kind of them, I think. And you must be grateful for all they done for you. I mean, caring for you, employing you in something useful, then sending you off into the world looking your best."

"Yes, sir. I was treated most kindly and I am appreciative of all they did for me."

"Have you had any breakfast, John?"

"No, sir."

"I'll tell you what. I've got some pork pie Mrs. Barnes just baked up yesterday and some good coffee. If you want to pitch in, I'll gladly share my grub. You can start by taking this bucket here and filling it from the wood-pile out back."

I do what Mr. Barnes asks. And while I do it, Mr. Barnes sets himself down at the teacher's desk, smokes his pipe and watches me. I fill the wood bucket, get the stove stoked and a blazing fire going. I retrieve a pail of water from the well, fill the washbasin and fetch another pail of water to have on hand. Mr. Barnes then sends me to scrub the privies, which I do until they are plenty clean.

When I've done that, Mr. Barnes says that's all I need to do. He knocks out his pipe. He then cuts two slabs from his big pie, and we enjoy it while sitting at the desks chatting about the old days when we both went to school. Mr. Barnes offers me a second piece. While I'm eating it, he sets to writing a letter. When he's done, he seals it with a clump of wax from the teacher's desk. He stands up. He tells me the teacher and students will be arriving shortly. I say I will be on my way.

"Have you got any money, John? I only ask because you polished off that pie like it's been some time since you've had a meal. And you've got a mighty small pack there to contain many provisions."

I shake my head that I don't.

"That's just about what I thought. I must admit, I had my doubts you could tote your skinny weight, par-ticularly when I saw those coveralls so fine and new. But you worked hard for your breakfast, and you worked like you're used to it. You also worked without a word of complaint. I don't know the story behind those ill-fitting clothes, and I'm not about to ask. All I know is they don't agree with all the rest. You've got those on, yet here you are sleeping in a schoolhouse, not in a proper bed. I'll let you in on something, John—I've run into more than one Home boy coming to this school. They come for a couple of weeks or months, and then they disappear. I've seen how they're treated by those who call themselves employers—it's shameful is what it is. That's why I'm inclined to give you the benefit of the doubt. Anyway, I'm going to recommend you to my sister. Mrs. Mabel Millard is a kindly soul and she runs a fine stopping house about twenty miles west of here. When you get there, you tell her Hector Barnes says you're a good worker and could she hire you for a few days to get you on your way. Her husband's working on the railroad and she'll appreciate the help." Mr. Barnes hands me the letter. "And if you will, pass on my warmest regards."

I tell him that I will gladly pass on his regards and that I am most grateful for his kindness. I keep my mouth shut about the coveralls, not wanting to go into the whole blessed story. Tucking the letter in my rucksack, I set out again.

Six

I set out across the windswept land west of the schoolhouse. There is no trail to follow, so I descend to where the Old Man River winds through a gulch of low bushes and snowbound weeds. Miles later, I have not come across a single horse hoof or boot print, not a scrap of evidence to convince me I'm not the only living being in this corner of the world. I guess this is partly what keeps me close to the lively trickle of water beneath the ice.

It's well past noon when I finally stumble across the first sign of habitation—a pony trail marked by day-old manure. Feeling a little less lonesome, I follow it, hoping it will eventually lead to the stopping house.

I have not gone far when I hear thrashing in the brush ahead of me. This is accompanied by the worn-out nicker of a hard-run horse. I skid down a bank and jump rocks to cross a shallow creek. It's around the next bend that I find the sorrel mare. She's still attached to her riggings, although there's not a sign of the wagon she was pulling. She's also managed to get herself all tangled up in the bushes and trees. It's my guess she's been snagged some time, because she's worked herself into quite a snit, and the shrubs are trampled to bits from her thrashing around. But for the moment—perhaps sensing me—she is still.

I whistle softly. Despite being exhausted, she looks over to where I stand. Her eyes are frightened, but she doesn't balk, and I can already tell she's been given no reason not to trust humans. Cautiously, I come around to her left side. That's when I see the good-sized welt across her flank. I suspect she somehow collided with the wagon she was hauling, bolted and broke free. However she received it, it's a day or two old, swollen up and festering. It has to be causing her some amount of pain.

"Easy, girl," I say. I begin to work the riggings free of the bushes, careful that she doesn't feel the tug. She's either an especially gentle creature or she's got no fight left, because she cooperates. It doesn't take me long to realize she's so entangled it's just about an impossible job to straighten it out. I'll have to cut her free. I approach her, speaking low and kind. She snorts and shudders, but she allows me to get close enough to cut her harness with my buck knife. Suddenly aware of her freedom, she darts ahead along the trail. A hundred feet ahead, she stops; it seems she's waiting for me to catch up. I take her by the reins and lead her to the creek, where she tucks in for a good long drink.

I do my best to wash the wound on her flank with cold snow from the edge of the creek, but it's going to need a good cleaning with Epsom salts to get the festering under control. There's no clue from the riggings where the horse might have come from. Once the mare has calmed down and cooled off, I lead her back along the trail.

She's a good, obliging horse, and I'd ride her if it wasn't for that nasty wound. But I have no idea how far we are from civilization, and I don't want to aggravate it.

We have been walking for nearly an hour before we run into another living soul. It's a small boy sitting on the railroad track. The moment he sees me, he shoots up and skitters down into the covert on the other side of the tracks. I scan the spot where he disappeared, picking out a pair of dark eyes staring up at me from the leafless bushes.

"Hello, mate," I say. "Won't you come out and talk to me? What are you doing all alone out here in the wilds?"

Realizing he is visible, the young Indian lad crawls from the bushes like a small animal. He is maybe eight or nine years old, spattered in mud and dressed in moccasins and animal hides.

"Some miles back I came across this injured horse. Maybe you can tell me who owns her?"

The boy shrugs. He thinks a moment before nodding.

"Good. Well, then, could you take me to where I might find him?"

He glances hesitantly over his shoulder.

"Do you speak English?"

Again, he nods.

"Well, where do you come from?"

"Down in that gully—in the trees," he finally tells me. "But we're hiding."

"Hiding from what?"

"The government." He wanders over and runs his buckskin mitten along the flank of the sorrel mare.

"Your folks are hiding from the government too? Well, how about that, so am I."

He looks up at me and grins. Clearly he likes the idea of coming across someone else who is hiding from the government. "Come on." Waving for me to follow, he starts along the trail.

As we walk, he tells me his English name is Henry. His Pikani name translates to Little Crow, if I care to call him that. I then begin to wonder what I've got myself into. I suddenly realize I'm not all that enthusiastic about the idea of meeting a tribe of Indians, particularly all alone, miles away from the civilized world. I had often seen them in Macleod, but I'd never actually had the opportunity to talk to them. All I know is that Buck had warned me that Indians were a warring kind.

Little Crow leads me to a clearing in the woods, to a very old, ramshackle hut, a soddie that has become overgrown and matted by the summer sun. The hut is now crumbling under the weight of the melting snow. It strikes me that it must have been built and later abandoned by one of the first families to homestead in the North-West Territories, maybe fifteen years before. It is of very old construction, with strips of sod stacked and supported by poplar poles.

I follow Little Crow into the clearing, where a girl who looks to be about my own age sits by a fire, absorbed in quill work, singing quietly to herself. I can hardly believe my eyes at first, she seems so out of place. She's just so pretty—it's like stumbling across a rose blooming in a field of mud. She wears a buckskin dress, and her long black hair is gathered at her neck, which is decorated with a brightly beaded neckband. When she sees me standing next to Little Crow, she jumps up, knocking over the quills in her haste.

Little Crow introduces her as his sister, Maddie. For a moment, she stares at me with the same owl-like concern that I'd seen in Little Crow's eyes. I guess she is wondering if I should be welcomed or turned away. She takes a few steps toward the soddie and speaks in her native tongue. A woman, who I guess to be Little Crow's mother, appears in the doorway. She cradles an infant with cheeks as pudgy as two custards. A man steps past her out of the hut. He is a most imposing figure in his worn robe of buffalo hide. He says something sharply to Little Crow, who immediately runs to his parents. Not understanding a thing of what is happening, I think of running too—in the other direction.

Little Crow turns to me. "My father wants to know why you are here. I have told him you are not an enemy and that you are also hiding from the government. He wants to know what you have done that they are after you."

I don't see any point in explaining my whole wretched history, so I tell Little Crow to tell his parents the same thing I'd told Cyrus Jones. That it was a misunderstanding. That I'm accused of doing something I never did, and I have no authority to prove otherwise.

Little Crow's parents listen with much attention. I don't know how much they understand of what I'm saying, but I do believe they recognize my way of speaking as being of a foreign nature to Canada. This seems to interest them. Finally Little Crow's father nods. That it's a misunderstanding appears a satisfactory answer to him. I'm relieved. Little Crow's father motions toward the horse.

"I've come to return this horse to its owner."

Little Crow translates. His father turns, raises an arm and indicates a point farther west. I look past the fire to where the bush opens onto a broad plain. Half a dozen cream-colored tipis, smoke rising above them, sit clustered in the distance. Women work above the orange campfires as small children and dogs mill about the camp. I spot a corral built of brushwood some distance behind the lodges.

"We'll take her to Willie Many Horses," Little Crow explains.

With Little Crow at my side, we leave the bush and approach the camp. The women straighten from the fires or look up from the hides they are fleshing. The small children run to clutch their mothers about the legs. Their wide eyes are on me as we walk toward them.

Little Crow leads the sorrel mare. I follow behind, past animal skins staked on the ground and racks of drying meat, toward the brushwood fence. Willie Many Horses is pitching hay from a wagon into the corral. Little Crow speaks to him quickly. He doesn't immediately react, so I tell him why I have come.

"Mr. Many Horses," I begin, "I was just passing through and I stumbled on this mare in the bush. She was all tangled up in wagon riggings. Little Crow here says she might belong to you. She's got a sorry wound across her flank. You'll want to see to it right away so it doesn't get any worse. I'd recommend cleaning it with salts and covering it in a clean plaster. Anyway, I've come to return her to you. I mean, if she's yours."

Willie Many Horses finally stops what he is doing. From where he stands on the haywagon, he looks down on us. He is a most striking individual, leaning on his pitchfork with his Stetson at a bit of a tilt. He wears beads and feathers laced in his long hair, and a number of amulets adorn his chest. His shirt is constructed of buckskin and ornamented with quills and tassels of weasel fur. He looks at the horse, but he still doesn't answer. Instead, he returns to forking hay.

He isn't the sort you'd want to badger, so I stand watching him for another minute, only because I don't know what else to do. I decide I'd better ask someone else.

"What's your name?" he asks at the moment I'm about to walk away. I'm surprised he speaks English.

"Charlie."

"Who's your employer?"

"I don't have one. Well, not anymore I don't."

This finally prompts Willie Many Horses to lay his pitchfork aside. Pinning his Stetson to his head with his fingers so it doesn't fly off, he jumps from the wagon. He stands before me, looking me over from head to toe. He then looks at the mare. She is nuzzling my hand. "How long have you been on your own?"

"About a week or so."

I'm not sure why I'm being interrogated. All I want to know is if he owns the horse or not. Either he does or he doesn't.

"Why did you leave?"

It's becoming a common question. "It was the result of a misunderstanding. Look, Mr. Many Horses, if this is your animal, I wish you'd take her. Or even if she's not, I'd appreciate you caring for her because I'm in no position to start asking around in search of her home. The fellow involved in the misunderstanding is going to be scouting around for me. I can't risk running into him, I'm just about starved and I'd just as soon get on my way."

I hear my own voice trail off. I hadn't meant to go on the way I did. I realize I'm not only wretchedly hungry, but I'm awfully tired too. I'll have to be more careful—start guarding myself against going completely barmy and slipping up.

Willie Many Horses doesn't ask anything more. Instead, he inspects the sorrel mare. He takes the reins from my hand and leads her into the corral. Willie says something to Little Crow, who takes me by the arm and begins to steer me back to his family's camp.

When we reach the soddie, Little Crow speaks to his mother, repeating some of what Willie Many Horses has said. She looks up from where she's preparing a meal by the fire, smiles and motions for me to sit. Maddie passes me a bowl.

They feed me roasted deer meat, prairie turnip and tea to warm me up. Rosemary—that is Little Crow's mother's name—bounces the baby on her knee and watches me eat with fascination. After every few bites, she leans forward and pinches my cheek. It's as if she thinks the food should be going straight to filling up the hollowness. When there appears to be no immediate improvement, she sits back, glances at the pudding-cheeked baby she jostles in her arms, frowns a little and pushes more food toward me until I can't possibly pack another morsel into myself. By the end of dinner I am surprised my cheeks haven't swelled right up simply from being pinched.

As we eat, I ask Little Crow why his family is living in the hut hidden in the bush, separate from the rest of the clan.

Maddie answers. And because it is in such a formal manner, I reason she and Little Crow must have learned to speak English from going to school.

"Mother and Father do not want Henry and me to leave the day school and go to the residential school off our reserve. Many children who have attended have become sick and died. They don't want Henry and me to die too. We left my father's family in the middle of the night because my parents received word a government official was coming to take Henry and me away." With a sweep of her arm she takes in the broad plain. "This is my mother's family. They are hiding us for now."

It makes sense their parents don't want them to go to school. Anyone with half a mind could figure that after many deaths it is only reasonable the school should be shut down and not reopened until the disease has run itself out. Even Albert Brooks in his worst state of drunkenness would not have put an infectious animal in with the rest of the herd. "How long have you been hiding here?"

"Since November. After our cousins, who were at the school, both took sick and died. It was very cold when we left. We're waiting for the weather to warm up before we make a more permanent home. And then there's the baby. He was born when we first arrived, and both he and Mother were very weak for many weeks."

I look at the baby swinging in his mother's pouch. If he was as weak as Maddie says he was, Rosemary sure has done a fine job of plumping him up.

"What about you, Charlie? Tell us your story."

I tell Maddie and her brother how I got to where I am. Little Crow can hardly believe I came to Canada all on my own, or that I have no kin. "Well, somewhere back in London I've got a brother and some sisters."

"But not one in this country?" he asks.

"Not a one," I say.

"Why'd you stay so long with the Brooks brothers?" Maddie asks me. "It seems to me you'd have been better off on your own."

She had no idea how often I lay on my straw tick, tossing and turning this very thought around. I tell her about the stories I'd heard of boys running off and ending up dead.

"So what now, Charlie? Where are you off to?"

"I'm told there's good money to be made working in the mines. I'm headed to the Crow's Nest Pass."

We play a game of shinny on the open plain. Little Crow is small and quick, and it's nearly impossible to stop him once he has control of the ball. By the time the sun is about to set, he's scored ten goals to our three. On the way back to the clearing, I rip my moccasin on a root. Maddie insists on sewing it up. I sit next to her by the fire, watching her wield the quill needle as easily as she handles a shinny stick. I'd taught myself to sew out of necessity, but I still never failed to stab myself every time I struggled to darn one of Buck's socks.

When Maddie is done, she smiles and hands me the mended moccasin. It strikes me again how pretty she is, and I also think she is very kind to sew up the moccasin for no other reason than to mend it for me. I have an urge to hug her, but considering I've only known her for a few hours, I'm not sure how she'd take it. I'm pretty sure I know how her father would, however, and so I don't.

I sleep that night in a corner of the hut on the softest, warmest bed of fur and hides. Before I leave, Rosemary loads me up with food that will keep: bannock and pemmican and dried saskatoons.

Little Crow and his father ask me to make a trip with them back to the corral. Willie Many Horses is already there, where he seems to be waiting for me. "I have a horse to give you, Charlie," he says as I approach. "You will travel faster with a horse."

I am so surprised I can't think of what to say. I stand between Little Crow and Willie Many Horses, leaning on the top rail of the fence. Willie points out a half-dozen horses in the corral. "Any of those would be suitable for you."

He owns at least forty: five palominos, a number of Arabians, seven handsome Appaloosas and some fine saddle horses. He even owns a couple of thoroughbreds. I am to pick the one I most fancy. I'm not sure why he is giving me a horse, but it's mighty kind of him. When I ask, he tells me it's a trade.

"But I have nothing to trade for it," I tell him.

"You brought me the injured mare."

I'm sure not used to getting the better part of any bargain—in this case, a horse for simply returning what Willie already owns. And if he doesn't own her, he seems to know who does, so I don't question or argue. Instead, I choose a quarter horse. A chestnut gelding.

"That one—he is a good one," he assures me. "You won't be disappointed with him. He's a calm, gentle horse, confident on the trail. You'll be glad of that when you're traveling through the Rocky Mountains. About twelve years old I'd guess him to be."

"You sure do own some fine animals."

"I have an eye for horseflesh," he says. "I have to. I have selective buyers. Now, I've got a bridle and a saddle here that's yours too."

It's early afternoon by the time I say goodbye to Little Crow and his family. I have a difficult time saying goodbye to Maddie. She's just stirred me up so I feel good inside. I thank Willie Many Horses for his generous gift.

It has warmed up considerably by the time I start out, and there is no call for me to wear my mackinaw. I tuck it between me and the saddle. The food I stow in what Willie called a parfleche—he'd hung the buckskin pouch from the saddle horn. He'd also given me instructions on how to get to Mabel Millard's stopping house by following buffalo trails so that I could avoid the more well-used trails.

West Coast Cody—I call my horse that because that's where we're headed—is as easy a ride as Willie said he would be. He is surefooted, responsive and willing, and although he is only a horse, being on the run is now not nearly so lonesome.

The snow on the trail is melting quickly, but since Cody and I are the only traffic, it's still in a passable state and there is little risk of getting stuck. We've been going along about an hour when something gets Cody jittery. He nickers and pulls back. At my coaxing, he continues along the trail, but he doesn't like where we're heading.

"Cody, what's got into you, boy?"

I put it down to something he's caught a whiff of in the air.

Seven

March 29, 1903

From the vantage of a bluff, I spot a settlement of some type in the distance. Fifteen minutes later, Cody and I are trotting through a camp—a cow-camp. By all appearances, the few tents have been abandoned in a hurry—even the chuckwagon has been left behind. After a more careful inspection, I decide it didn't happen recently. The tents have collapsed from the weight of snow, and the wheels of the chuckwagon have had time to sink into the earth.

I've come across cow-camps before. There are plenty around because a herd can only be moved ten to twelve miles in a day. But usually only the plank floors for the tents remain. And if the cowboys are on a drive, staying only one night, they often don't even bother with tents. They roll themselves in their blankets and stretch out beneath a wagon or a canopy of prairie stars. I can't tell what it was just by looking, but something chased these cowhands out of this valley. I lift the canvas and look beneath. It appears they took nothing but the clothes they were wearing.

Their personal items—their soaps and washing flannels, even their straight razors—were left behind.

I open the drawers and compartments of the chuck-wagon, pulling out what there is on hand: a crock of sourdough, coffee, beans and tins of tomatoes, stewed prunes and beef. There are also plenty of cooking utensils, so while Cody crops a few hearty tufts of grass rising from the snow, I set about making a stew. I also brew a pot of Arbuckles. Good, strong, cowpuncher's coffee.

After I've eaten, I sit on the cook's stool and look over the long, empty valley while enjoying my coffee and a smoke. I'd come across a tin of Turrets in the chuckwagon and rolled myself a cigarette. It's sure a sight—those hills spotted with jackpine—a magnificent sight, but lonesome as well. Not a creature stirs as far as I can see but for Cody. He's settled down some. The scent of whatever he'd caught earlier probably carried right over the valley and away from his nose.

I clean up my mess, dump snow on the fire and stir it around to be sure it's out. I don't take anything but food, not wanting to root through any of the personal stuff. Cody starts out more cooperative. It isn't until we reach the top of the next rise that he starts balking again. Cocking his ear to the right, he whinnies and snorts low. I really have a time keeping him to the trail. I also have trouble keeping the meal I've just enjoyed in my stomach. The stench of death hangs thick and sickly in the air.

Jumping off Cody, I lead him from the front so as to give me better control. I nearly land right on the cause of the smell. I look down—my attention caught by the slight jingle of a spur disturbed when my weight strikes the ground. The spur is attached to a leather cowboy boot. Inspecting it more closely, I leap back. I just about lose my lunch on the spot!

Lying face down beneath the low branches of sagebrush, and newly exposed by the receding snow, is the corpse of a cowpuncher. His Carlsbad, soggy and gray, still covers the back of his head where he lies. He is dressed in a long yellow oilskin slicker and heavy winter clothes; long johns poke out the cuffs of his trousers, and he is wearing woolly chaps. Cody is real edgy, so I walk him away from the body and hitch him to a tree. For several moments I lean against the tree myself. It takes some concentration to get a grip on my stomach as well as my nerves. I wonder at my run of gruesome luck—stumbling on another dead body in less than a month.

I return to the body of the cowboy. Because of the odor it is difficult to get too close, but I am curious how he died. Covering my nose with my sleeve, I hold back the branches overhanging the body. I bend down and look him over, but I can see no signs that he's come to his end in a violent way. There are no bullet holes or knife wounds in his back. I search for a lever. After finding a branch, I pry him up enough to be able to see him from the front. He is plastered all over with mud and twigs, and his gloved hand still clutches his lariat. But I can find no wounds on his chest or what is left of his face. I lower him to the ground again. By all appearances, it looks like he'd been walking along and fell to the ground face first. For whatever reason, he was unable to get up again.

As I am obviously the first to come across him since the snow melted, I feel an obligation to tell someone. I decide to tell Mabel at the stopping house. In the meantime, I don't have the means to bury him. Besides, he is in a fragile state, and I don't want to start moving him around in case he doesn't hold together. I also figure the more natural he is, the more likely those searching for him will be able to identify his remains. So I cover him in a pile of branches and leaves. I then lash together a cross, but before I leave, I think I should say something to mark his passing. It wouldn't be right to just bury a man without saying a considerate word. I have no idea what to say. I obviously don't know anything about him. Then I remember something John, the Carsons' farmhand, said. It was one day the previous August when we'd all been working in the fields: Albert and Buck, John, Mr. Carson and me along with the men hired to do the threshing. Albert had struck me on the head for something. I can't even remember what it was, but that doesn't play into it.

Once Albert walked off, John had come up beside me. "Charlie," he'd said, "those boys are mighty nasty to you and we all know it. But someday you'll be out of this situation and on your own. Until then I advise you to live by a few words from the Code of the Range. This is how the cowboys manage their lives because theirs is not always such easy riding either. They work hard and get knocked around a lot, like you. The two cowboy commandments you'd be wise to pay heed to are these: You got to say little, talk soft and keep your eyes skinned. And don't argue with the wagon boss. If he's wrong, he'll find out."

I understood the first part all right. I'd been keeping my eyes skinned since the first time I'd been whipped. It just took me a minute to figure out that by my wagon boss, he meant Albert Brooks.

Remembering all of this, I take it upon myself to make a eulogy for the man lying beneath the leaves. I figure a suitable tribute to a cowboy would be recognizing that he'd lived his life the way it was laid out in the Code of the Range. "Here lies a cowboy who said little," I begin, "talked soft and kept his eyes skinned. And he didn't ever argue with the wagon boss. Rest in peace."

I hammer the cross into the ground with a rock. I unhitch Cody and start down the trail again. Twenty minutes later we emerge from a wooded area at the top of a ridge. I glance down into the coulee to the west. It's a sight to soften the toughest cowboy's heart.

Laid up on top of each other, decomposing in the sun, are the bodies of a hundred or so cattle. Winter kill. Free-range animals that had wandered into the coulee when it was filled with snow to escape the bitter cold. Here, they had huddled together for warmth. But unlike the cowboy's corpse, they do not give off the smell of rotting flesh. If these animals hadn't frozen to death, they had surely starved. The drifts had set in and they'd had nothing left to forage. This meant they had no muscle or fat to stink when they decomposed because they were nothing but skin and bone when they died.

The corpse and the abandoned cow-camp now make sense. The cowboys had been attempting to drive the herd in where they'd be safe from the bitter cold. A blizzard swept in and they were lucky to save themselves—except for the dead one, who probably lost his way and, much worse, his horse.

I whistle for Cody to move on.

The land is much hillier now; it no longer rolls out so that you can see miles in the distance. Snowdrifts are receding from the floor of the heavily timbered valleys, and jackpine dapple the bare hills. In places I lose sight of the trail. I trust Cody to follow it with his nose.

It's coming on dark by the time we arrive at Mabel Millard's stopping house. I tie Cody to the hitching post out front. There's a livery out back, but I think it best to approach Mabel Millard before I take the liberty of putting Cody in the barn. I have to walk around a pig-pen to get to the back of the house. A large black sow, ornery as they come, follows along on the other side of the split-log fence. She screeches and grunts at me, complaining that she doesn't like me walking anywhere near her. The foul smell of a turkey house reaches my nose. The sow's complaints get the turkeys flapping and fussing, so that before I even reach it, Mabel Millard comes to the kitchen door to see what all the fuss is about.

"Lucy, stop that caterwauling," she demands of the hog.

Mabel Millard is a big woman with a handsome face, even though she is as old as Hector Barnes. She wears her silver hair pinned in a coil at the back of her neck, and a worn but starched apron covers her gingham dress.

"Mrs. Mabel Millard," I say, "my name is John. John Laurier."

Mabel Millard does not appear nearly so kindly as her brother had made her out to be. She frowns as I speak, causing me to take a step back.

It dawns on me to take out Hector's letter. "I pass on warm regards from your brother, Hector Barnes. He suggested you might be able to give me a place to sleep and a meal for a day or two, in exchange for some work. I can do just about anything."

Mrs. Millard takes the letter. She inspects the seal, breaks it open and reads. To my relief, she smiles in an approving way. She has all her teeth, and they show nice and even. She looks me over again and begins to laugh. "How some things don't change. Hector always was the one to save a bag of kittens from a drowning. Come on in, young man. But it isn't John. I know it to be Charlie."

My heart takes a tumble. I can't think of what to say after hearing my name.

But Mrs. Millard takes me by the arm and pulls me into the kitchen. "Don't you worry. I'm not about to put stock in anything Buck Brooks has to say. His reputation precedes him as one to take advantage where he can. That fella would turn his own mother in if he could get a nickel for it. I've had more dealings with him than I care to admit, haggling over feed prices in Pincher Creek. He was through here about an hour ago. Looking for an unsightly Home boy by the name of Charlie, skinny and evil-minded."

Again, I am stuck for words. But I'm not as disturbed to hear Buck's still looking for me as I am that Mabel picked me out from that description.

She laughs again. "Skinny and evil-minded were Buck's words. Now, Charlie, are you starving? How about some mulligatawny. Then I'll introduce you to my nephew, Roland. Not Hector's boy, but the son of another brother who was killed many years back digging a well. Roly runs the livery and will put you to work. You can bunk with him for however long you stay. I sure can use the help with my husband working on the railroad."

I thank Mabel Millard for her kindness. I dig into that mulligatawny while she pours a kettle of water into the wash basin and cleans up from her guests. I can hear them talking down the hall.

"Three families heading north," she tells me. She wipes her hands on her apron. "Let me show you around and take you out to meet Roly."

Mrs. Millard leads me down the hall to the sitting room, where the families are gathered. The room is set up with entertainments for those stopping in for a meal and a bed. For seventy-five cents a traveler gets an evening meal, a mat to sleep on and a bowl of porridge with salt pork before setting out the next morning. Mabel also keeps a store stocked with things that those traveling might need: canned goods, bicarbonate of soda, licorice all-sorts for fussy children, and needles and thread for quick repairs.

On our way to the barn I tell her about the dead cowboy. She says he must be the fellow gone missing in a January blizzard—up from Montana. Just as I thought, he'd been lost as the men tried to round up the drifting cattle. After I tell her the approximate location, she says she'll pass it on to the Mounted Police. We walk past the travelers' wagons, loaded down with all that they own. Roly is inside the barn, organizing horse tack. He's already brought around Cody, who is happily munching hay.

"That chestnut gelding yours?" he asks once Mabel introduces us.

"Yes, sir, he is."

"He's of mighty fine breeding, handsome, sturdy and calm. You must have paid some amount for him."

I don't say one way or the other.

"Roly here loves his horses," Mabel tells me. "But you can see that for yourself. Look how well cared for they are."

Roly Barnes is around about thirty years old, pleasant and even in nature. He is most generous in sharing his quarters in the bunkhouse next to the barn. He sets me up a bed and a small table beside it where I place the contents of my rucksack, including *The Pilgrim's Progress*. Once I'm established, he picks up the book, looks it over and asks if there is anything else I might need. I say no, that everything is just fine.

The next day, I help Mabel in the kitchen by keeping the woodpile stacked and the stove stoked, washing dishes and peeling vegetables. I also work alongside Roly, cleaning stables and feeding and grooming the horses. He does his share, always helping out when a job is bigger than one person can do. Roly is friendly and he talks to me like I have some brains about me, always explaining why he does things the way he does. But I can't help feeling that something is bothering him. I pick this up from how his mind wanders off in the middle of a job we are doing, or how he gets a few words into a sentence and forgets the rest of what he is about to say.

I discover what's plaguing him two days later. We're sitting around the bunkhouse playing cards in the evening—Roly has won the final hand. We square up, with me owing him one more stall to clean out. I pull off my moccasins and lie back on my bed. After knocking out his pipe, Roly strolls across the room and picks up *The Pilgrim's Progress* where I'd left it on the table. He's picked it up a few times since I arrived, each time turning the pages, frowning and placing it down again. This time he holds on to it.

"Charlie, can you read this?"

I nod. "I have. Many times when I was at the Brooks."

This seems to get him thinking. "How about writing? Can you write, as well?"

"I can. Maybe not as clear as some."

Roly sets the book down and sits at the end of my bed. "I'm wondering if you'd do something for me. If you'd write me a letter. See, I haven't been to school since my dad died when I was twelve years old. That was when the well he was digging caved in on him. When he was gone, I had to step into his shoes. Anyway, what it comes down to is I can't write or hardly read myself, and besides, I'm not so good with words."

I shrug. "Sure, I can do that. What kind of letter do you want me to write?"

Roly presses the palms of his hands to his knees. "I want you to write a letter asking Olivia Newbold to marry me."

Every afternoon, Roly drives the hay wagon two miles along the trail to the Newbolds, a neighboring farm. This is where he buys feed for the livery. The Newbold family appears to include at least a dozen children—Olivia is the oldest of the brood. She is ten years or so older than me, with broad shoulders, and she wears her blond hair down her back in a long, thick braid. On the two afternoons that I've accompanied him, she's rushed out to greet us, smiling widely at Roly. Today she passed on a basket of eggs, and a jar of preserves she made herself. Yesterday it was a jar of the most delicious tomato relish. It was like nothing I'd ever tasted in my life.

So it isn't so much a surprise that Roly wants to ask Olivia to marry him. It's the way he decides to go about doing it. "But Roly, why don't you just come out and ask?"

"Because I can see she's the sophisticated sort. She'd think higher of me if I could write it out. Charlie, I'm thirty-one years old and it's time I got my own place. I need a wife; someone kind and warm who will raise my children and help work my land. A man just can't do it on his own. I've seen the results. I don't want to mess up my chance. That's why I want you to write it how it should be. Besides, I don't know as I have the courage to ask her face-to-face."

"But I don't know the first thing about asking someone for their hand in marriage. I can write it, if you want, but you'll have to tell me exactly what you want to say."

Roly marches over to the table next to his bed and opens the drawer beneath. The supplies I need have already been placed close at hand. "Here's ink and a pen and a sheet of Mabel's writing paper. I don't think there's anything else you'll need." He moves the lamp in closer to illuminate his little table. He then begins to pace back and forth with his hands thrust deep in the pockets of his dungarees as he thinks about what he wants to say. "Sit down, Charlie. Okay? I'll start dictating. Good, okay. I'll begin. Dear Miss Olivia. How's that for a start?"

I sit at the table, dip the pen in the ink and write. "Dear Miss Olivia. It sounds as good as anything to me."

"Okay. I'll continue then." Roly ponders a moment. "Seeing as how I'm of a mind to start my own place, and you're of stout body and, I dare say, sound mind, with a good knowledge of cooking, laundering, gardening, caring for children…"

I put the pen down.

"Aren't you going to write this, Charlie?"

"I will if you want. But Roly, like I said, I don't know anything about courting or marriage, but those don't seem like the right words to be starting off."

"Why not?"

"Well, this kind of letter—I mean, if you're trying to woo someone—it just seems to me that you shouldn't start off with naming chores and things."

"But those things are the important ones. What should I start with then?"

"I'm not certain, but I think it should be more—complimentary. Like the way Mr. William Shakespeare would have wrote it. Okay, here's an example. There was one piece of poetry I read in school where he compared his sweetheart to a summer's day. Can't you think of something Miss Olivia Newbold reminds you of? Something nice, like a summer's day? We could start out with that."

Roly thinks about this. "Yes, okay."

I pick up the pen again, preparing to write.

Roly thinks a moment longer. "Dear Miss Olivia," he begins. "Seeing as how I'm of a mind to start my own place and you remind me of Lucy…"

I put the pen down again. "Roly, you can't compare Miss Olivia to a hog!"

"Why not?" Roly appears thoroughly frustrated. "Lucy *is* something nice. She may be a little ornery, but she farrows the strongest litters we've ever had. We've never lost a one in all her years of producing."

"That may be so, but you still can't compare her to a hog."

Roly drops to the edge of his bed. He rests his head in his hands for a moment, leans forward and speaks to me in an earnest way. "Charlie, Olivia Newbold is used to children. She's raised all those brothers and sisters herself while her mother was out helping in the fields. She's used to this land, its coldness and the swarms of mosquitoes in summer. I don't want a wife like some are advertising for in the East. I want one that knows what to expect. Someone who's not going to hightail it out of here the first time she gets a blackfly bite or gets whomped on the head with a nugget of hail; someone who won't holler 'cause she's up to her ankles in mud after it storms."

I dip the pen in the inkstand again. "Okay. We'll just say it straight out with no extras."

Roly nods.

"'Dear Miss Olivia,'" I begin. "'Seeing as how I'm of a mind to start my own place, I am judging it to be about time to take a wife. I am admiring of the way you raised your own brothers and sisters, and I certainly enjoy the preserves you prepare. I particularly find your tomato relish most delicious. Therefore, I would be honored if you would consent to marriage with me. I will be awaiting your reply at the livery at Mabel Millard's stopping house. Yours most sincerely, Roland Barnes.' There. How's that?" I hand the letter to Roly.

He studies my writing with a mixture of confusion and awe, nods and folds it up.

Eight

The livery barn is a busy place, what with people coming and going. Besides boarding horses, Roly has two Belgians by the names of Samson and Delilah. He also keeps a couple of Indian ponies and rigs for rent. In one corner of the barn he allows ranchers to display the wagons and farm implements they are wanting to sell. It's a good place to advertise, because those heading to their homesteads might find something they need to get started. Roly gets a small commission for his trouble.

Toward the end of my second week at the stopping house, I am laying fresh straw in the stalls when a cowboy comes in looking for a secondhand saddle. Roly lays out what he has. Judging by the way that cowboy handles those saddles—tossing them aside like corn husks as he disapproves of one after another, cursing and declaring them worthless—I gather him to be an unpleasant sort.

"I ain't interested," he finally says.

Roly and I look at one another. I know Roly has another couple in the bunkhouse, just brought in from

Pincher Creek, but I gather he feels the same as I do about the nature of the man. He has no inclination to tempt the cowboy to stay any longer. "Well, I showed you all I got. Sorry I couldn't help."

But instead of turning around and leaving, the cowboy strolls right past him into the barn. He stops in the center of the room, strikes his heels into the dirt and squirts a jet of brown tobacco juice at his feet. His gray beard is streaked with it. He wears rawhide chaps that are thick with mud, and his bandanna is stained with sweat. In answer to Roly, he grunts. He then begins to scan the stalls on either side of the barn, walking between the two rows with his spurs jingling, closely inspecting the horses that catch his interest.

"I showed you all the saddles I got," Roly tells him. "If you're interested in a horse, these belong to our guests. I don't have any for sale at the moment. Only the two Indian ponies at the end there are for rent."

This doesn't stop the cowboy. He continues to check the occupied stalls.

"Listen, cowboy, I'm manager of this here stopping house and livery barn you're standing in, and I don't like strangers eyeing what belongs to my guests. Just what is it you're looking for?"

"I'll know it when I see it."

He stops in front of West Coast Cody's stall. Cody, normally of mild temperament, shies away. He balks and snorts at that cowboy and won't let him come within ten feet of him.

"Where'd you get this one here?"

"Hey!" I drop what I'm doing and quickly run over to Cody. Roly is already at his stall. He shushes me with a look.

"This horse belongs to a guest. A Mr. J.D. Harper. A gentleman with distinguished taste."

"I can see that. Perhaps you can tell me where I might find this Mr. J.D. Harper." The cowboy's mouth twists as he spits out the name like it's left a bad taste.

Roly draws himself to his full height. He is a broad-chested man of not less than six feet with another two inches of black curls and a sturdy cowboy hat on top of all that. "I'm sorry, but Mr. Harper has retired. He is not feeling well and asked specifically not to be disturbed."

The cowboy can see Roly is not about to budge. "Well, you give Mr. J.D. Harper a message for me. You tell him Mr. Richmond Longhurst of High River is going to want to talk to him."

"I'll pass it on. When the opportunity presents itself."

The cowboy nods. We watch until he's mounted his horse and is some ways down the trail.

"Charlie, where did you get West Coast Cody? You've got to tell me."

"I can't. All I can tell you is he was a gift."

"Come with me. I want to show you something."

I follow Roly into West Coast Cody's stall. The horse is calm now, trusting us to inspect him. Roly strokes his head while he points to the brand on his left flank.

"Look here. Does this here look like the brand of the man who gave you the gift?"

I don't know what to say. I had noticed the brand, but

the truth of it is I hadn't noticed if all of Willie's horses had the same one. I shrug. "I wouldn't know."

Roly sighs. "Let's just hope Mr. Longhurst doesn't come looking for Cody himself."

Mabel pays me fifty cents at the end of each day for my work, on top of providing me with room and board. I think she is most generous. I tell this to Roly as we finish the chores before closing the livery that night.

"Mabel has a big heart, and we've both been glad to have you helping out over these past couple of weeks."

I start thinking about the nearly seven dollars in my rucksack. It's more than I've had in my entire life. I then think about how I'll be able to make that in only two days if I get on at one of the mines in the Crow's Nest Pass.

"Do you think they'll take me on at the mine?" I ask Roly.

Roly sets his pitchfork aside. He takes a long draw on his pipe before pulling it from his mouth. Since Olivia had accepted his marriage proposal, I'd noticed he now went about his work with an easier mind. "Well, you're not much in size," he tells me, "but you work twice as hard as most men. You've just got to get them to give you a chance to prove your worth, that's all."

I finish straightening the saddles the cowboy had tossed about as I determine that's what I'm going to do. Three dollars a day is more money than I can imagine. If I can get on at the mine, I'll easily save enough to go down to the land office in a year when I'm somewhere about eighteen.

On our way to the bunkhouse, Roly lights his pipe again and starts talking about me staying on for good. I could run the livery for Mabel after he and Olivia are married, and once they've moved to a place of their own, I could come visit for Sunday dinner and spend Christmas with them and their children.

"You already know everything you need to know about feeding and caring for horses. I can see you've had a fair amount of experience in the past. Mabel really likes you, Charlie. She likes the way you work and how fast you figure things out when you don't already know them."

I don't tell him I had to get quick at it when I was at the Brooks in order to save my hide.

I consider what he's said. "I don't know, Roly. You and Mabel have been awfully good to me. And I'd like to have dinner with you on Sundays and Christmas with you and your children. But I need to put more distance between me and Buck Brooks. I'm sure to run into him again if I stay around here."

"Won't you at least think about it?"

I tell him I'll think about it over the next few days. But it's less than twelve hours later the decision is made for me.

I'm cleaning stalls in the livery just before noon when Roly comes tearing in. "Charlie, the cowboy's back. And he's got five men with him. I just spotted them coming down the trail. You've got to tell me right now—where'd you get West Coast Cody?"

There is no point keeping it a secret any longer. I'm not sure why I had anyway. I guess I suspected what Roly is about to tell me, and I'm embarrassed to admit it. "Willie Many Horses gave him to me."

"Willie Many Horses!" If I'd said any other name, it couldn't have got him more alarmed. "Charlie, he's a notorious horse thief! How did you ever come about getting a horse from him? He pinches only prime stock. Sneaks them off right under a rancher's nose. Nobody can figure out how he does it. No wonder they got a policeman with them."

"They've got a policeman? Roly, I've got to go!" My nerves get me flying faster than a sparrow from a hawk. I tear out of the barn and into the bunkhouse to collect my rucksack. I stuff in my few belongings.

"You stay right there," Roly calls after me. "I'll talk to them first. You'll have to give up Cody, but they won't accuse you when they hear where he came from."

I race back to where Roly stands next to Cody's stall. "Roly, you don't understand. They're not going to care about Cody once they know who I am. I don't have a chance against Buck Brooks. I've got to go. I thank you for everything, and Mabel too." I have a hard time not tearing up as I take a last look at Cody. I start for the door.

"Charlie!"

I turn around.

"If the Mounted Police really believed Buck Brooks, don't you think they would have tracked you down by now? They'd have your description stuck in every post office and train station across the North-West Territories.

They'd have their men scouring up and down these trails. I haven't seen a one, and I'd never heard mention of you until that good-for-nothing came barreling through Mabel's door."

For a very quick second I think about what Roly has said. "That may be so. But I can't take a chance by staying around. I've got no one to fight for me if there's any doubt. Besides, even if they're not thinking I'm a murderer, I'm still legally bound to work for Buck by the agreement of the Home. I'm a runaway, and I just can't go back. It's best I clear out of here altogether. That's why I'm heading west."

Roly can see there is no holding me back. Moving quickly, he begins saddling West Coast Cody. "Well, if I can't stop you, you're sure not going to make it all the way on foot. Not through the foothills and most certainly not through the Rocky Mountains." After leading Cody from the stall, he passes me his reins. "Take him. Come on. You don't have a chance without a horse. You get on him, and you take that buffalo trail out there behind the livery—follow it as far as it goes. It's about an hour before it meets up with the trail from Pincher Creek. At that point you'll be close to Bellevue, and just down the trail from that is Frank. Once you're in town, you'll blend in with all the other foreigners come to work in the mines. You tell the livery where you board Cody that you worked for Richmond Longhurst at one time. That'll stop any questions.

"I can't believe I'm doing this." Roly is sweating something awful. "I'm a partner to Willie Many Horses.

Charlie, you got me a wife and you turned me into a low-down horse thief at the same time. You get going, now, do what I say. I'll stall them by telling them J.D. Harper was feeling more himself and moved on, headed down to Montana. It'll take them a few days to trace him to the cemetery where he lies next to my dad."

Despite my desperateness, I laugh.

I step into the stirrup and swing up onto Cody's back. Roly leads him to the door, where he peers into the yard. With all clear, he starts him off with a smack to his rump.

Nine

The terrain is rocky and uneven as Cody and I make our way along the buffalo trail. The gentle rise and fall of the plains is long behind us, but Cody is surefooted as he picks his way over the stone outcroppings. Now and again I drop my hand to the small wad of shinplasters in my pocket. As the distance grows between me and Mabel's, I have to keep assuring myself that my time at the stopping house and the wages she'd paid me weren't all just a dream.

It's awfully hot for the beginning of April. I suddenly remember that I've forgotten my mackinaw, which I haven't worn in more than a week. Roly had given me a linen shirt to replace my heavy flannel. He'd also passed on a pair of trousers so I'd have a choice of something to wear. The trousers were too small for him, but I have to cinch them with a piece of doubled-up twine so they don't slip off my waist. The rope is chafing in the heat.

After a time, the trail descends through thicker brush, and I can see only as far as the next bend in the path.

Every so often we pass a trail leading off from the one we're following. A dozen feet in, these animal paths disappear into even denser bush. There is no sign of human life. Cody wades across a stony creek, and a few miles along, another. Or perhaps it is the same one and has just changed course.

After riding in silence for some time, I begin to miss Roly and his talk. Without paying much attention to the trail, I begin thinking about how I don't have a kin or friend in the world. A pitiful lad I am, a fugitive from the law, cast out on his own in a harsh, foreign land. I'd had a wretched childhood, that is certain; an orphan torn from his siblings, sent on a ship to a strange place, only to be dreadfully mistreated when he arrived. But it isn't the ruggedness of the land or the hard work that weighs so heavily on me—those things have been difficult, but tolerable. Even my poor diet hasn't killed me. It's the loneliness and not belonging that's so hard to take.

Oh, sure, some might be worse off than I, but I can't think of many. Okay, maybe that fellow Joseph Carey Merrick, the one they called the elephant man. I'd seen old bills posted in London advertising his deformity as entertainment—born so grotesque he was treated as a creature, not human, and made into a sideshow freak. But other than him, I can think of no one else who's had an existence as sorrowful as my own.

I have quite convinced myself I am the most unlucky lad in the world, when I look up. I've been so absorbed in feeling sorry for myself that I haven't noticed how low the sun is getting in the sky. Roly had told me I should be meeting up with the main trail within an hour. I've been traveling now for more than two. I whistle for Cody to stop. I listen beyond the sound of him softly snuffling and stamping. I don't hear the rumble of carts or wagons, or the hooves of horses, not a note that would suggest we are nearing the main trail. A branch snaps. I scan the woods, but I can't detect anything. It must have been a heavier animal moving somewhere off the path.

I am now quite certain we've taken a wrong turn. I try to keep the rising knot of fear pressed down in my stomach. I've lost all sense of direction, and I can't see clearly through the trees to what is left of the sinking sun.

I search for something to focus on, to get my bearings again. I hear another snap. I remember the fresh coyote scat farther back along the trail. But this time, I am sure of it, the snap is followed by a faint metallic sound. Not a sound any animal would make. The surge of panic creeps further up my throat.

We go on another fifteen minutes. I heel up Cody after making a turn in the trail. I jump to the ground and just stare at what lies ahead. We are about to travel through a broad valley marked by a wide river and, to the east, a railroad track. On either side of that valley, the Rocky Mountains rise higher than anything I've seen in my life. There is no mistaking it is them. If I'd discovered them first, I wouldn't have named them anything different. I watch as tufts of clouds drift lazily, obscuring the white peaks. I can hardly believe we've done it. We've made it. I want to whoop and shout! But Cody has worked up a sweat and is in need of water. He is restless, wondering why I have just stopped and am staring at where we are headed instead of making an effort to get there. I climb on his back and start down the trail again. Cody takes a sudden dip to his left and I now see that he is hobbling. Jumping to the ground, I lead him along a path that winds down to the river.

While Cody stops for a drink, I begin to rub his leg, working my way down the hock to check his foot.

"Looks like he's lost a shoe," says a voice behind me.

I whirl around. The voice belongs to an old fellow with a tangled beard and a gnarled face. And if there is a soul on this earth who is dressed poorer than me, or whose circumstances have affected his physical appearance worse than mine, this is him. His clothes are thin and full of holes, and they hang on him like he's shrunk three sizes from the day when he first buttoned them up. When he turns, he makes a soft clanging sound. I look down at the collection of snares and animal traps dangling about his waist. He takes a step forward and tips his battered hat.

"It's the left hind one seems to be giving him some concern. But not so much that it's painful. Just a little off-kilter. I watched you coming down through the woods. Mind if I take a look?"

I manage to pull my eyes from his unfortunate appearance and nod. Cody is agreeable, and the old fellow is absolutely right. I am thankful it is nothing more serious.

The old man straightens. "Well, son, it will be dark in an hour and you'll not make it to Frank before the blacksmith's gone home for the night. You can come back to camp with me. I'm just down the river. I'll cut the hoof level with the sole so it doesn't break off. You can get your horse to the smithy first thing in the morning."

I'm not sure what to do. I can't even guess the intentions of this wiry old trapper who followed us down through the woods. My experience with Cyrus Jones is still fresh in my mind, but I'm also concerned about my horse. Cody *had* warmed to him. I don't see that I have a choice. "I'd be grateful to you, sir. I don't have either nippers or rasp."

"Good." His hand shoots out to shake my own. "My name's Andy Grissack. And you, lad? Your voice tells me you're a long way from where you were born. What are you doing in these parts?"

I have no strength to go into a long explanation. "My name's Charlie Wittecombe. I'm looking to get a mining job in Frank." I'm about to stop there when I remember what Roly recommended I say. "I've spent the last few months working on Mr. Richmond Longhurst's ranch."

When I'm finished, Mr. Grissack holds off asking any more questions. I'm grateful for this as I'm suddenly wary he might be familiar with Mr. Longhurst and his ranch. Instead, his eyes meet mine with some curiosity before he breaks into a grin.

"Well, Charlie, I happen to know the pit boss, Edgar Ash, in Frank. And if I know Edgar, before he'll even look at you, you're going to need some plumping up. Once we get your horse looked after I'll cook you up a stomachfull of bacon and beans that ought to put some ounces on that slight frame of yours and give you a better chance." He begins walking along the river, indicating that I should follow.

I look ahead at Mr. Grissack, all gnarled and knotted, and I think it a bit odd that he would make an issue of my being so slight. But I'm not so clever I can out-judge a man who lives off the land in a climate so harsh. I've also worked up an appetite since setting out from the stopping house.

Mr. Grissack isn't a formal man, and he insists I call him Andy. I lead Cody along the soft part of the riverbank as we walk a mile or so farther down to his camp.

Andy lives in a tent both summer and winter. The skins of beaver, wolf, fox, muskrat and marten, scraped and hung to dry, flap near a smoldering fire. Behind the tent is a paddock where he keeps his own little Indian pony. A rough shed for tools and supplies leans next to the rail. Andy disappears into the shed, returning with the tools he needs: a hoof knife and rasp. He also brings a clinch cutter and pincher to remove the right hind shoe for balance.

Andy Grissack doesn't need my assistance, so while he trims the hoof, I turn toward the mountains again. I've had trouble pulling my eyes from them. They are a spectacle like I've never seen before, and they keep drawing me back.

Andy looks up from his work. "Charlie, you look like you've never seen a mountain in your life."

I shrug. "Well, I guess that's a fact. I haven't ever seen a mountain, except from a distance. I've seen places that were named like they were mountains, but now I know the people who named them couldn't have ever seen the real thing."

Andy lets Cody's foot down and stands up. He nods. "That one straight ahead—they call it Turtle Mountain. Right at the foot of it, a bit to the west, lies the town of Frank. And that over there, that's Goat Mountain. And the lights over that way, they belong to the ranch house of my neighbor, Mr. James Graham. Him and his wife and two sons run a dairy. They're good folks to an old trapper. Come on, now, we'll finish up here, feed these horses and get ourselves something to eat."

The warm day cools off quickly once the sun disappears behind Turtle Mountain. We leave Cody and the Indian pony happily munching hay. Andy lights a lamp in the tent and stokes a fire in the stove. I thank him for looking after Cody and comment he must have had some practice at what he'd done.

Andy chuckles as he works open a tin of beans. "I've done more than just trapping in my long life." After slicing some portions from a chunk of salt pork, he mixes everything into a black pot and sets it on the stove to warm.

Aside from the stove in a corner of the tent, there is Andy's cot, a willow rocker that has worn grooves in the wooden floor, a small table and two thatched chairs. Andy motions for me to sit while we wait for dinner to cook.

He drops into the rocker and lights a pipe. "Yessir, I do more than just trapping to keep alive. I know every creek and crevice in these mountains; I've followed them from the rivers they feed back to their beginnings and learned them all. I've packed my pockets with gold dust, and I've pulled some real handsome nuggets from these creeks. Tell me, Charlie, you ever hear tell of a man named Bill Lemon?"

"I can't say that I have."

"Well, I'm going to tell you a story about Mr. Bill Lemon while we wait for our dinner to warm." Andy takes a long pull on his pipe as he prepares to tell his story.

It's all about a prospector by the name of Bill Lemon, who came up from Montana in 1870 with another prospector named Blackjack in search of gold. The two came across a lode in these parts, but in a fit of greed Lemon killed Blackjack. He then went crazy because of his crime. Many fellows have since searched for the mine—but every one of them ended up either crippled or dying. Some say it's because the mine is cursed.

When he is finished his story, Andy knocks his pipe against the chair. As I wonder why he has told me all this, he stands up and stirs the bubbling pot. "So, what do you think, Charlie? Do you think the mine is cursed?"

I shrug. "I can't say. I mean, I don't know anything about it except what you just told me. But it sure does sound like it from the story you tell. All those who go looking for it end up taking sick or dying. But you would think that in thirty years it would have been found. Maybe it's not real."

"Oh, it's real all right. Like I told you, I've plucked some nuggets the size of your eye out of those creeks. But besides all that, I can feel it right here." He presses his free hand to his chest. "I just know it to be so."

Andy ladles out a good helping of beans onto two tin plates. After passing one to me, he sits on the edge of his rocker again. "See, I don't believe in curses. That's what separates me from those who've given up. There was a time when dozens of men crawled through these parts looking for the Lemon Mine. But those got scared off by accidents and mysterious happenings. Not me. I'm trading muskrats and beavers for my bacon and beans right now, but I'm aiming to live out quite a comfortable old age."

He still hasn't told me anything that actually proves the mine is real. Maybe Andy Grissack thinks that if he believes hard enough, it will make it so. But I'm not about to dispute the word of the old trapper. It will do nothing to benefit me, and I suspect he's already heard enough discouraging words, living on the edge of civilization all alone as he does. Instead, I wish him luck in finding it. We talk on for a while longer, I thank him for dinner and we turn in for the night.

I sleep by the campfire on a heap of pelts. Andy says he could easily make room on the floor of the tent, but I decline. The air is warm as bathwater, I tell him, and it has been months since I've been able to sleep under the stars. The truth is, I'm not quite ready to bunk up in such close quarters with an old fellow I've known for only a couple of hours.

The clatter and clang of mine machinery carrying across the valley in the chill air wakes me the next morning. Mist hangs heavy in the hollows, and a fine layer of frost clings to my cover and the surface of the tent. My nose feels as cold as a chunk of ice. I sit up and rub it as

Andy throws open a flap of the tent. The fire is going and he appears to be already on his way somewhere. His tools, traps and gold pan swing freely from his waist, clattering into each other, and over his shoulder he carries an empty burlap sack.

"Morning, Charlie," he says, seeing I'm awake. "I'm on my way to check my lines. Got to do it early, so I can put in the rest of the day looking for my mine. There's plenty of coffee and biscuits on the stove. I'd advise you to take your horse to the livery you'll pass on the way into town. It's where the mine horses are stabled, but Robert Watt will be sure to do the work. Mention you know old Andy Grissack."

I thank him for all he's done.

Andy Grissack stands facing Turtle Mountain, adjusting his braces and the sack over his shoulder. But before he leaves, he says something else. "Charlie Wittecombe, it really doesn't matter what life you come from out here. If it was a fancy one, or if it was poor. You'll find most folks in this part of the world are coming from something they'd rather leave behind. It's the one thing that makes us all the same."

I nod. I then watch the old man hobble along the river to discover what he's caught in his traps. I wonder what Andy Grissack left behind before coming to this part of the world. I also hope that this will be the day he finds his gold and gets comfortable, because it seems to me that he's already living out his old age.

Once the sun is up, it turns into another warm day. There is a fresh breeze blowing as Cody and I set out along the wagon trail heading west. I know we have to be nearing Frank by the amount of traffic coming our way.

We first come across a dozen tents pitched in the valley next to the railroad track. Men move about carrying picks and shovels, so I guess it to be a construction camp of some type. The next building is a cabin with a business at the front, a shoe shop. And a little farther along, the smell of horse sweat and leather tells me I have to be coming close to the livery barn.

More than fifty horses are stabled at the mine livery; some do dray work, but most are used for hauling coal. Mr. Watt isn't in. His assistant, Francis Rochette, tells me all this. He is a friendly fellow and most accommodating. I can leave Cody with him and he'll have him reshod by noon. Mr. Rochette then asks where I'm from and where I'm headed. I tell him the same as I told Andy Grissack.

"I've been working for Mr. Richmond Longhurst from High River. I'm now looking to get work in the mine."

Francis Rochette wishes me luck. "But the fact is, Charlie, there's no shortage of experienced fellows coming in from overseas. But who knows, they might need someone to help with the timberwork. Mr. Watt, my boss, is a carpenter in the mine. He says they're always shoring and replacing the support timbers in the tunnels. Seems to be a bigger job than in most mines. But I'll tell you what—if there's no work for you there, you might try one of the hotels. They're always bustin' with business, what with the miners from Hillcrest and Bellevue, and the construction crews. Then there're the cowboys and the trappers and the drifters coming in for a drink, a game of blackjack or a bit of feminine companionship."

"I'll remember that," I say.

Francis directs me to Dominion Avenue, Frank's main street. I start out on foot along the trail. To the east, a half-dozen shacks sit scattered across the flats. Following Francis's directions, I turn down Alberta Avenue, where I pass a row of miners' cottages—seven in all. Once past the cottages, the path jogs before crossing a bridge over Gold Creek. It winds through a rough-cut clearing of rocks and stumps where it meets up with Dominion Avenue. Except for Turtle Mountain looming over it, it looks like most main streets I've come across in the territories. Wooden sidewalks separate the false-fronted buildings from the dirt road, which with all the melting and freezing is chewed to mud.

Frank is not even two years old, but already the shops and services most folks need to be comfortable have sprung up. I stroll past the Alberta Mercantile Company store, the post office, the Union Bank and the Imperial Hotel. Everything is new and hastily built, yet the town has a rough edge to it, like it isn't quite used to itself.

It's still early in the morning, but the street is already busy with people going about their business. Silk skirts rustle as women hustle squealing little children between shops. Horses bray, and now and again my ears are jarred by the shriek of ungreased wagon wheels. Boot spurs jingle and barkeeps holler at one another across the street. They're out on the sidewalk, sweeping up the dregs left behind from the previous night: spilt liquor and spewed chaw. In front of the Frank Hotel, I pass fellows speaking in words more foreign to the territories than my own. And some not too far different—I recognize two voices as fellows from Wales.

Those milling about the street wear all manner of costumes: sheepskins, tweed jackets, fur leggings, wool stockings, Stetsons, turbans and high-laced boots. In many of the faces I recognize the bluish tinge of coal ingrained in their skin from years spent working underground. I'm not the only fellow who has found his way to Frank, drawn by the prospect of three-dollar-a-day wages. These fellows come from coal pits all over the world.

But the best part is nobody pays me any mind. For the first time since I've been on the run, I blend in with the queer collection of voices and clothing. On my way past the bank, I stop a gray-haired fellow to ask directions to the mine office.

He wears a green felt cap and is moving stiffly, like his legs are full of rheumatism or his bones have been broken and healed all wrong. His thick neck and face are raw and crimson, and his hands, when he waves them toward the mountain, are big and square.

"To the end of the street and across the creek," he manages to say before bringing his fist to his mouth as he is overcome with a fit of coughing. I offer to do something for him, run and get some water or something—it seems it's tearing up his insides. But in the midst of his seizure he manages to shake his head. It finally ends when he spits a black patch on the ground.

I thank him and start up the street toward the mine.

Ten

"I know I don't look like much," I tell Mr. Ash in the mine office. "But I'm strong as any mule. I pick up on things fast too, so I won't take much training. You've just got to give me a chance to prove myself, that's all."

Mr. Edgar Ash leans back in his chair, waiting patiently as I rush through my words. When I'm finished, he smiles, but he shakes his head. "Well, lad, I would give you a chance if I could, but we aren't hiring. All I can do is suggest that you try again in a few weeks. Are you planning to stay in town for a time?"

I nod. I mean to show that I'm serious, but I also haven't thought of what else I might do.

"All right. The weather's turned and I'm expecting to lose some fellows to the fields. Summer's our busiest time, with the railroad stocking up on coal so they can move the harvest in the fall. Leave your name and check back with me at the end of the month." He stands up. "Maybe I'll have something for you by then."

I tell him I'm grateful for his consideration and he

won't be sorry. I then write my name in the ledger. For my residence, I put the town of Frank.

Outside the office, I look over the property belonging to the Canadian American Coke and Coal Company. Across the Crow's Nest River are piled heaps of coal, mounds of rock waste harvested from the picking tables, and stacks of timber to shore up the mine. The pit head is maybe thirty feet above the river at the base of Turtle Mountain. Men work around the towering mine tipple, where the hoisting, dumping and screening equipment is housed.

A train engine backs down the mine spur, headed toward the tipple across the bridge. Two miners stand next to the track, waiting to hook up the hoppers. The engine clangs along the track—brakes squeal as it backs up to the cars to be coupled. I turn and head toward Dominion Avenue.

After crossing Gold Creek, I pass a boarding house for men working at the mine. Perhaps I'll have a chance of getting room and board there once I'm taken on. In the meantime, I have to find a way to live. My wages from the stopping house will not hold out for two weeks. I then remember what Mr. Francis Rochette said about the hotels.

The Frank Hotel has no positions available. I continue down Dominion to the Imperial Hotel, where I speak to Mr. Ruben Steeves. I tell him I've heard he runs a booming business and suggest that he might need help. He looks at me skeptically, but he doesn't say no right away, which gives me some hope. Folding his arms, he rocks back on his heels.

"Well, son, tell me what you can do."

"Anything," I quickly answer. "I can do whatever you've got that needs to be done. I can work in the kitchen, chopping, cleaning and washing dishes. Or I can wait on people if you have a need there. I can split wood and scrub floors. I'm most versatile."

"Can you boil sheets and launder linen?"

"Yes," I say, "I'm practiced at doing that too. I did all the laundry at my previous employers'."

"And what about scouring basins and slopping cuspidors and chamber pots? Can you hold your stomach with those kinds of chores?"

"Yes," I tell him, "I can."

"Good. I'm afraid you wouldn't be much use if you couldn't—not in this business, anyway." Mr. Steeves eyes me a little longer. "Well, I do need someone around at night to clean up after the men have left the bar, to mop the floor and such. If you're willing, come back at seven o'clock tonight and I'll try you out."

I can hardly believe my good fortune. I want to rush forward and shake his hand. Instead, I thank him and leave the hotel to collect Cody. With a lightness in my chest I'm hardly used to, I walk to the end of Dominion Avenue. I wind around the stumps and rocks in the clearing, cross the footbridge and walk past the row of miners' cabins along Alberta Avenue. Cody is wearing new shoes when I arrive at the livery. I pay Francis Rochette and thank him for the suggestion of applying at the hotels. He asks me where I'm planning on staying.

"'Cause if you don't have a place, it's common for fellows to set up camp in the valley across the trail, past those temporary shacks on the eastern flats next to the river. I've got some old tarps here you're welcome to use. They've got a few tears in them, but for the most part they'll keep the weather off. You can fashion them into a tent and you'll be fine until your pay starts coming in."

It's a fine idea and will allow me to use what money I have to feed myself and stable Cody. I set off toward the eastern flats with the old brown tarps folded across Cody's back. I balance an axe across my lap, also loaned to me by Mr. Rochette.

Once I leave the wagon trail, I head south across the valley directly toward the base of Turtle Mountain. Frank is expanding rapidly, and Francis Rochette had explained that the shacks I'd be skirting—ten in all—were thrown up to accommodate mine workers and their families until more substantial structures could be built. Once I've passed the shacks and am nearing the river, I come across the campsite. Tents of all manner and sizes are scattered through the valley and along the river's edge. I search for a spot to set my own. I scout out a flat spot near the river, but bordering a wooded area where I can hunt for poles.

It takes me a good part of the afternoon to search out and cut the proper length of poles. I then have to figure the best way to fashion and attach the tarps. After tearing a narrow strip off one of the tarps, I rip it up further into long, thin strips for guy lines. I build a frame to position the tarps across. I'd acquired a couple of shirts from

Roly, so I see no cause to keep the originals I'd got at the Home. They're shrunk up to my elbows and scrubbed right through in places by lye. I put them to better use by tearing them up and using the scraps of fabric to lash the ends of the frame together.

When I'm done, I stand before my patchwork house, thinking it's about the ugliest place a person could live. And not all that sturdy. One good wind and it's likely to be carried off to end up fluttering from the mountain's peak. But it's mine. I can cut a window in the side if I wish and nobody can holler at me or tell me different. I can invite Cody in for a nip of oats if it strikes me as something I want to do. The final thing I do is dig a small pit for a campfire, the way the others have done.

Once I'm finished, I stand and survey my surroundings. My closest neighbor is about thirty yards away. His cook fire is cold and his new white canvas tent is tied shut. Mine looks like a weatherworn little dory next to his set of shining sails. I haven't seen him about yet.

I look in the other direction. A Chinaman stoops outside the entrance to a very poor lean-to fashioned from branches and a tattered oilcloth. I glance at my own tent again. The Chinaman's lodgings are even more humble than my own. He's squatting in the dirt, scrubbing his clothes in a tin pan. He stands up. It's when he turns sideways to hang a pair of trousers over a branch that I nearly gasp. He's dressed all in black and he's dreadfully thin, even thinner than I am. He moves in a very deliberate way. It appears to take him a great deal of effort just to lift the tin pan off the ground. I watch him carry it to the woods and dump the suds. By the time he's walked back, sat next to his campfire again and got his pipe lit, he seems just about all tuckered out.

I decide to ride into town and see about boarding Cody at the public livery. I'm awfully hungry and I plan to also pick up some bacon, coffee and beans. I start down the wagon trail. On my way through the village of tents, I pass my Chinaman neighbor. I nod, tell him good day and introduce myself. His mind seems already occupied, but he does make the effort to look up, return the nod and tell me his name is Ling Yu. He drifts back to his thoughts and pipe again. I remind myself to be sure and offer him some bacon and beans when I get back.

If I have to be without friend or kin, I decide, this is the way life should be: looking after only me and my horse, nobody knowing who I am or accusing me of crimes I didn't commit. Mr. Alex Leitch, proprietor of the mercantile exchange, is pleasant and doesn't even blink at the way I speak when I ask for my salt pork. And because there's all manner of strange costumes around, nobody turns to look at how ill-fitting my clothes are when I pass them on the street.

I leave Cody at Mr. A.P. McDonald's Livery. After returning to my camp on foot, I get a fire going and fix my supper. I take my first mouthful and feel my stomach warm. It makes me think of skinny Mr. Ling Yu, who I remember must be starving. Looking across to his camp I see that his fire is out, and he doesn't seem to be about. Maybe he's gone into town in search of something to eat. I finish my meal, then have a smoke while I sit by the fire, running the day's accomplishments through my mind.

The sun is beginning to settle behind the mountains. My neighbor in the white tent has returned to his campsite and he's now setting about making his own supper. He waves to me as he stokes his fire. From a distance he doesn't appear to be much older than me, but he walks with the weary gait of a chap who's been doing physical labor, lifting and hauling weights much greater than his own. There is a great hiss and whoosh of smoke as I pour water on my campfire. I stir it up and set out for the hotel.

Mr. Steeves wants me to start my evening in the saloon. I'm to wash dishes, keep the stove stoked and make sure the dice and cards are on hand for those who want to play. Once the bar closes and I've scrubbed it clean, I'm to help in the laundry, boiling the sacks of sheets and linens. I'm also to assist the porter, when called upon, by carrying baggage and taking horses round to the livery. I'm to blacken boots left outside the doors and make sure that those leaving town are up in time to catch their train. My shift will be over once the fancy passenger train, the Spokane Flyer—the train that runs between Lethbridge and Spokane—has pulled out, about four or five in the morning. My wage is seventy-five cents a day.

The saloon is blue with smoke. Miners, navvies, lumbermen, trappers and ranchers are gathered along the length of the bar. The air is mighty pungent, a powerful brew of human and horse sweat, tobacco and beer, all tied up with the aroma of manure tracked in across the floor. Mud and coal dust from the miners' boots also blacken the planks.

As I clean spills and pick up dirty and broken glasses, I'm aware that the language around me is coarser than what's heard on the street. But it's still not so coarse a preacher couldn't listen in. It's only as the night wears on and the fellows make a game of treating one another— buying shots of whiskey and tossing them back—that the talk grows rough, tempers rise and those inclined to griping get harping on whatever is weighing on their minds.

"Just step aside, Charlie," Mr. Steeves warns me. "Don't get in the way when the fellows get heated up or you're liable to get your chin broke. They don't always see who they're swinging at when they're full up with whiskey and mad at the companies they're working for."

He doesn't need to warn me; I'm already keeping my head low. I've had plenty of practice at recognizing when fists are about to fly, many thanks to Albert Brooks. But I do ask Mr. Steeves what they could be so mad about.

"Oh, lots of things. The men in here have plenty to keep them on edge." He sets the drinks he's carrying in front of his customers before he stops to explain.

"Now, let's see, those over there are miners. Those men spend ten hours a day in a pit without seeing the light of day. Besides accidents with machinery, they've got to worry about getting crushed beneath the earth, flooded out or poisoned by gas. They work in a place where a fella just striking a match to see what's before him could touch off an explosion."

I nod toward another group across the room.

"Those boys—those are the navvies. Building the railroad is deadly work as well. They aren't stuck underground, but they pay for the meager food the company feeds them by way of lost limbs and crushed bones. Their living quarters aren't fit for humans; the men are packed twenty-five or more into a boxcar like they weren't even people, but rats."

Mr. Steeves is about to tell me more, but a game of pitch and toss is turning ugly. One fellow says the other won by stepping over the imaginary line.

"In a pig's eye!" the fellow accused of cheating barks. "I won fair and square. And who are you to be calling me a cheater—you're the dirtiest chiseler here in this room! There's nothing lower than stealing from your own. Now give me what's owing and rightly earned."

The accuser refuses. He's awfully offended at being called a chiseler, and he answers by curling his lip and cocking his fists. The men standing around do nothing to discourage the fight. Instead, they seem to do everything to encourage it. One group sides with the fellow who claims to have won—echoing his words that they are tired of being taken advantage of. There are plenty enough folks around wanting to swindle them—they should at least be able to trust their own kind. The other group supports the fellow who accused the other of crossing the imaginary line.

"Those boys aren't from around here," Sam, the barkeep, tells me. "They're from one of the mines farther west. That fellow's the check weighman. He's responsible for making sure the company weighs the coal proper and the miners get their due. Some say he's been taking bribes and the men aren't getting their full amount. Obviously there's some agreement with that belief."

The chap accused of cheating his fellow miners takes the first swing. But the two get only a few blows in before Mr. Steeves calls for help. Between him and Sam and the porter, they manage to get the two brawling men out the door and into the street, where they are left to slug it out in the mud.

It isn't the only fight that night—it's just the first that breaks out. Some fellows come into the bar, toss back a couple of shots and are on their way again. Others arrive from their shift and stay all night. They're the ones who get so full up with liquor they're lying out on the slag heap of a floor by the end of the night. It's my job to help rouse them and get them out the door at closing time. Sam doesn't seem all that concerned about what happens to them once the door is closed.

"They'll sleep it off out there in the road. At least until Constable Leard carts them off, or it starts raining and their nostrils fill up with mud. Or if they have a woman, she might come looking for him and haul him home. Not many do, though, or they wouldn't be passing their time in here. There are three fellows to every woman out here in these territories. Now, Charlie, you get the floor scoured. I'm going to close up."

I scrub the scum and ashes from the counter and tables. The floor is almost as disagreeable to clean as the old sow Lucy's pen. Some of the railroaders had taken it upon themselves to play a game of kick-the-old-spittoon. At the same time, they'd continued to employ it for its intended use.

Once that's done, I find the laundering room. The laundress, a woman by the name of Violet Love, is not much more than five feet in height, as plump as a barrel, with skin as pale as plaster. I guess her to be around about forty years old. She stands above a roiling pot, boiling linen in a room where the walls and windows drip with sweat. Her heavy black hair is pinned on top of her head. When I appear in the doorway, she looks up from her work as she pushes a strand of loose hair from her damp brow.

"So you're Charlie." She continues to plunge the linens in the pot with a paddle. More hair comes lose and falls forward into her eyes. "I was told to be expecting you. Mr. Steeves says you already know how to launder and press. I sure do hope so 'cause I don't have the time to be training inexperienced ones and get my own work done too. Come over here, lad. You can take over what I'm doing while I wring that batch out over there."

I step into the room. The rush of steam into my lungs momentarily stifles my breath. Violet hands me the wash paddle. I can't help but notice that her bare arms are covered all over in raw patches of skin. Right up to her elbows. I guess it's from having them always dipped in suds and lye.

She's a hard worker, but her work doesn't require that she pay it a lot of concentration, so at the same time as she works, she likes to talk. She asks where I'm from and what I'd done there. I tell her the same as I've told everyone in Frank—that I'd worked as a ranch hand at Mr. Richmond Longhurst's ranch near High River. But owing to the fact that he'd lost a good part of his herd in the harshness of the winter, he didn't need me anymore. I don't like telling the fib over and over. Instead of getting easier, it is getting harder to tell. But I can't be trusting everybody I come across. Not on first meeting them anyway, and not after my experience with Cyrus Jones.

Violet's worked at the hotel for nearly a year. She has five children at home to care for, but she needs the wages; her husband is a miner who lost a foot when it was crushed beneath a runaway railcar.

"At least they kept him on," she says, twisting a sheet, squeezing out the last few stubborn drops. "They took Peter out of the ground and put him on the picking table, where he makes a pittance compared to what he did setting off blasts. Still, I know I should be grateful. Many fellows aren't so fortunate. If they lose an eye or a hand, they're done for. If they make it out alive, that is. They're told there's nothing left for them, and they leave with nothing to show for their work but their crippledness. I tell myself it's for the best anyway. What with all the strange goings-on, I can't say I'm not glad he's out of the pit."

"What strange goings-on would those be?"

Violet is through all her squeezing and wringing and is now plunging the next batch of sheets I'd washed in the bluing kettle. "The fellas have been feeling bumps; they say the whole mine quivers and rocks like it's been struck by a ship. Then there's talk of the upraises where the coal's been mined that have mysteriously closed overnight. It's no secret that coal mines itself—the coal falls with little help from shovels and picks. Some fellows have quit, fearful the whole pit's unstable and there's a disaster building."

"Do you think there is?"

Violet shrugs. "I can't say. Peter says there's always a disaster brewing if you really want to think about it. Not only natural ones from mining, but ones the men brew up themselves. You just never know who's sneaking matches and cigarettes into where they're working. They hide them in their boots or behind their ears so's the fellows searching them before they go into the pit can't find them. I guess what he means is you can worry as much as you want about what the mine's doing, but you really never know what direction the next catastrophe will be coming from. No sense wasting precious time worrying about it. I suppose he's right. But it's still no argument to prevent me from being concerned. He's not the one that would be left with five gaping mouths to feed." Violet wipes the suds from her hands on her apron. "Charlie, why don't you run that bundle through the mangle and peg them on the line."

I squeeze the last drops of water out of the sheets by feeding them through the two rollers of the mangle. I then load up a basket and carry the sheets outside. The air is cool on my face, most refreshing after that swampy room. When I return, it takes another two hours to get through the table linens and bath towels. As the night wears on, Violet begins to wilt from the heat until she finally loses her voice and just works. When we are done, she sends me to black the shoes while she dumps the soapy pots and finishes up.

The early morning air is chilly when I leave the hotel an hour later. The sun is not up yet, but there is a pink glow spreading across the eastern sky. I shiver in the cold; I miss John's old mackinaw. Hiking up my collar, I burrow my hands deep in my pockets. Dominion Avenue is just beginning to stir. Hay wagons and ox carts clatter over the half-frozen ruts as men arrive from neighboring farms for supplies. Mr. Sam Ennis's coal dray clambers past before turning down Second Street. The Graham's dairy wagon is stopped outside the Palm Restaurant and Bakery.

Men and boys pass me on their way to the mine. They appear from different directions; they come from the miners' cottages in the west part of town and they come from the eastern flats. They fall into a line once they are on Dominion, filing toward the base of Turtle Mountain. They walk with a slow but steady gait, some suffering from old injuries and pains, others stiff with muscles still half-asleep. Some wear canvas coats, while others shiver in lighter clothing, like me. They all wear patched trousers, boots and leather caps and carry their lunch tins strapped to their backs. I look after them, thinking how they look like a line of insects as they march toward the train bridge. After crossing the Crow's Nest River, they'll be swallowed up in the great clanging beast of a mouth.

Alberta Avenue is quiet as the miners' families continue to sleep. Francis Rochette is outside the livery, brushing down a pit pony. Robert Watt is readying horses for the drivers on the way to the mine, fitting them with harnesses and helmets.

The smell of cook fires and coffee brewing is inviting as I walk across the eastern flats. The tents that are closed up must belong to the men who are already at work in the mine. But there are plenty of fellows sitting around eating breakfast, doing their washing or just having a smoke. These fellows are either looking or waiting for work.

I'm dead tired. I've been up nearly twenty-four hours, but I feel good as I fry myself some bacon before I turn in to sleep. The sun is rising, and I can feel that spring is about to stay. Once I've eaten, I roll a cigarette and finish my coffee. The warmth of the sun on my face and the freshness of the air remind me of walking behind Duke and Duchess, breaking up the earth after it has thawed. It was the one chore I would never have traded with Buck or Albert, even if one of them had insisted on taking it over. This is so fantastic a thought—that either of them would insist on taking over a chore—that I chuckle.

But I am sober again just as quickly when I realize Buck can't possibly manage the plowing and planting on his own. Roly may have been right—Buck may have been forced to give up looking for a murderer—but with so much work ahead, he won't give up looking for me and holding me to the contract of the Home.

Eleven

April 11, 1903

Coal cars bang across the river, jolting me as I take a last drag of my cigarette. It makes me think of the fellows I'd passed on their way to the mine, and how they'll be spending the next ten hours in the dark passageways beneath the earth. I remember my conversation with Violet and I start thinking that perhaps someone snuck a match in and today there'll be an explosion. Or maybe someone will lose a foot or an arm when a wall of rock caves in.

I rinse out my coffee pot. I have to stop thinking like that; there are lots of miners that nothing ever happens to. Why would anything happen today, or to me when I start underground? Besides, there aren't many jobs where you can make wages of three dollars a day. And I only plan on doing it until I've saved enough to buy my own land.

The fancy white tent next to the woods is closed up again. Recalling the fellow who had appeared all stiff and bent the night before, I figure he must be employed at the mine. I look toward Mr. Ling Yu's lean-to. His fire is also out and there is no sign that he is around. The trousers he'd hung over the branch to dry have blown off and are now tangled in a bush. Before I turn in, I walk over to rescue them. Crouching with the trousers draped across my arm, I call into the lean-to, "Hello in there."

A big fellow wearing a woolen shirt and sheepskin waistcoast is returning from the direction of the river. He totes a bucket in each hand. "You're wasting your breath," he tells me. "You ain't going to get an answer from in there unless you got a knack for hearing ghosts."

I look up, not certain if he's talking to me. "What do you mean?"

He stops walking, cocks his burly head to one side and sets the buckets down. Water sloshes onto the grass. "You mean, you don't know?"

"Don't know what? I just got here yesterday. I was working at the hotel all night."

"Oh, well, then you weren't here. That Chinaman fellow's passed on. Found last evening cold in his tent."

I think I must be so tired I'm not understanding him properly. "What do you mean, passed on? I saw him doing his washing around about suppertime."

The man shrugs a little. He has no explanation himself.

I'd spoken only a few words to Ling Yu, yet all of a sudden my stomach aches. In a way, I think it's my own fault. I should have right away given him something to eat when I'd thought of it, when I'd seen that he was in such terrible need. If I'd given him something to build his strength, he wouldn't be dead.

"Well, now, it's a terrible thing, son, but don't look so glum. It's not like it's your fault he slit his throat. He had his troubles. Even if you'd known about them, they weren't anything you could have fixed."

A worse chill than anything I'd felt in the dead of winter runs over my skin. I can hardly get my voice to work. "He slit his own throat?"

The big man nods. "It wasn't much of a choice—but I guess he thought it was the only one he had left. An Irish fellow across the camp knew his story. He'd worked on the railroad with him until they were both let go after the ground froze. This one here couldn't get work. He wandered about asking, but no one would have him. He'd been camping in the valley for near a month now, trying to get on at the mine. I don't know what he was living on, to tell the truth. Must have been scratching some sort of existence out of the earth. But the Irishman said what really seemed to keep him going was the thought of his wife and kin coming over. He'd been living on his own for nearly three years. His wife and two brothers were planning to come as soon as they could save the capitation tax. Well, the Irishman says he just about went out of his mind last week when he heard the government was raising the tax to five hundred dollars on every Chinaman's head. They may as well raise it to a million, they're about as likely to get it, the Chinaman told him. He wasn't prone to talking much, and after that he didn't talk again. The Irishman figures that's what did him in. With the government wanting that much money, his wife and brothers would never be coming. And even if there was anything for him in China, he would never have been able to raise the money to go home. Not in twenty years."

The man telling me all this waves toward the trousers in my hand. "Those belong to the dead man?"

I nod.

"You may as well keep 'em if you have the need. Others have already scavenged through his belongings and taken anything of value. I don't think there was anything, to be sure. He didn't even own a pair of boots. Don't know how he ever expected to get on at the mine. There was nothing but a few utensils, that knife he used, a pipe and a tin pan."

I can't do much else but stare at the trousers in my hand. I have an urge to throw them into the lean-to and run. I glance toward the opening. The man with the buckets sees me looking.

"Don't worry, lad. The Mounted Police were out and he's been taken away. It was cleaned up best they could. Maybe someone who doesn't care what happened in there will move in." He bends to pick up his buckets. "By the way, my name's Evan Kostos. I'm just down the river, closer to the mountain, if you're in need of anything."

I thank him. He nods and moves away. I drape the dead man's trousers over the branch I'd seen him hang them on the previous day. I don't know what else to do but try and get some sleep. Inside my patchwork tent I spread out my old bedroll on top of a piece of tarp. I lie there for a long time listening to the snap of fires, the distant hammering of the mine machinery, a horse nicker,

131

and the rise and fall of a dozen different voices. I turn on my stomach and reach for my buck knife stowed in the rucksack my head is lying on.

Feeling the coolness of the bone handle in my palm, I must have drifted off, because the next thing I remember I'm struggling to get it from the grip of Albert Brooks. I was dreaming I was back in my loft, where I'd come across him rooting through my belongings.

I wake up to the smell of dinners cooking and a darkening sky.

The valley is a busy place in the evening. Once the men return from their work, they set about gathering wood and water to cook their suppers. Those who have spent their day swinging a pick or loading coal sit on the ground with their boots off, eating from their tin plates. A fine dusting of coal still clings to their temples or beneath their chins, giving them the appearance of being in the shadows. Throughout the valley, the coughing and hacking of men clearing their lungs of the poisonous stuff is a common sound. After they finish their evening meals, they talk and smoke quietly among themselves, or they pull on their boots again and head for the saloons.

Outside my own tent, I poke up my fire. While I wait for my supper to warm, I look over the scene of weary, slow-moving men. The oilcloth covering Ling Yu's lean-to is gone—someone must have decided it would be useful. The trousers I'd hung over the branch have also been claimed. A fellow is now bundling the remaining branches for firewood.

I am still watching him when I hear footsteps come up behind me. I turn around. My neighbor from the white tent is approaching my campfire. Now that he's close up, I can see that, although he *is* only a few years older than me, he's taller and certainly more sound. He wears a corduroy cap, denim trousers and a heavy canvas overcoat.

"Good evening," I say, feeling just about naked in my thin set of clothes next to his warm ones.

He tips his cap. "Good evening to you, mate. It's a fine one, isn't it? What's your name?"

I don't say anything right away. Instead, I just gape at him and grin. After three years, I can hardly believe it! I've met up with someone nearly my own age with a voice the same as my own. The only thing that could have made me happier would have been if it was my brother Jack. I grasp his hand and shake it, more enthusiastically than I suppose the circumstances require. "It's Charlie. Charlie Sutherland." I don't even think to fib about it. Why would I lie when I'm practically talking to kin?

"Hello, Charlie. My name's James Tuttle. I must say, it's rather nice to meet another chap born within the sound of the Bow bells."

"Yes, it is," I agree, laughing. "It most surely is."

James smiles again before nodding toward the man toting away the bundle of branches. "It's an awful shame about that Chinaman, don't you think? A chap like that, coming out here to an unknown place, determined to make a living no matter how harsh the land. I bet it never entered his mind that it wasn't the land he'd have to most worry about. Anyway, makes a fellow really think about what's important in life. So, what are you doing here in Frank?"

"I'm looking for work. I'm on my own and I'm planning to eventually set down roots. I'm hoping to get on at the mine."

James nods. "Like most of the men camped in this valley. I'm working there myself. They've been shuffling me around, putting me where I'm most needed: oiling tubs, loading timber and cleaning lamps. The last few days I've been working as a duster. I've been with them two months and I expect I'll stay about two more."

I can hear my supper sizzling and spitting away in the pan. It's going to burn if I don't attend to it. I have to be leaving for the hotel in less than an hour. James has already eaten, but when I ask, he says he would be most obliged to join me for a cup of coffee. Once the water boils, it occurs to me that I only own one cup. I offer it to James, but he insists I keep it. I'm the one who's going to be needing a good strong swig of coffee if I'm to be working all night. He goes back to his tent for his own.

When he returns, he pours his coffee and squats on the ground across from me. "Tell me about yourself, Charlie? How did you get here? To the territories, I mean. Where have you been?"

"Until mid-March I was working on the Brooks brothers' farm north of Macleod."

"No, before that. Where is your family? When did you come over?"

"My parents are dead and I don't know what became of my sisters and brother. I come from Dr. Barnardo's Home." And while James sips his coffee, and I finish preparing my supper, I tell him my story as far back as I can remember. It's interrupted only when I sit down and take some time to chew. Or sometimes James stops me with a question: Do I have any idea where Jack might be? Was Drunken Alice any sort of kin? Why would the Brooks brothers treat me like that?

"So, are you still on the run?" he asks when I'm finished. "I mean, do you really think the Mounted Police would take Buck Brooks at his word? He sounds like a terrible scoundrel to me."

"I don't know if they'd believe him about me killing Albert, but they could make me go back to work for him on the farm. I'm legally obliged to do it too. So if it's all the same to you, I wouldn't mind if you kept my story to yourself."

James laughs. "You have my word, sir. You know, Charlie—you and me, we have a lot in common. Besides both being from London. Dr. Barnardo is my benefactor as well. I was given up as an infant. Given in to the castle at Hawkhurst. I lived in three foster homes. Last year, Mr. Blackmore, at the Home, told me I'd been selected to go to Manitoba. He said I was a good candidate to be working the land. I've spent the past eight months at the Industrial Farm in Russell, where they teach all about farming. I'm on my way now to work my own homestead." James smiles proudly as he pats his coat pocket. "I've been to the Dominion Land Office and I've got the deed to my own land right here. It's west of a village called St. Albert."

"Well, my heartiest congratulations," I say, offering him my hand. "Born into poor circumstances without a family to lead you, you are now to be a gentleman farmer in the territories. I am mighty pleased for you, James."

And I *am* pleased for him. I'm also now tremendously hopeful. If he has managed it, coming from circumstances not too different from my own, perhaps one of these days I'll save enough to accomplish it too.

"Thank you. I am pleased as well. I'm working at the mine for the money to buy a horse and provisions. I have a small amount saved, and I plan on staying until the end of May. I'll spend the summer breaking sod. When winter comes around again, I'll try and get back on at the mine, or maybe on a road construction crew." James gets to his feet. "Anyway, mate, I must let you go to work." He takes a last swig of coffee. "Tomorrow, Charlie, I have the day free. Perhaps after you get some sleep we could go for a hike. They say it's a fine view from the top of Turtle Mountain, and I have yet to see it. What do you say we tackle it?"

I say I'd like that very much.

It's Saturday night and the hotels and saloons are full up. Besides the regulars—the miners, loggers, railroad and construction crews—farmers and lonely homesteaders crowd into the Imperial Hotel. A fiddle dance at McIntyre's Hall is drawing crowds as well.

I make my way past four ladies gathered on the board-walk outside the hotel. They are the fancy type, waiting to conduct their business once the fellows have their fill of liquor. They coo and chuckle while making arrangements to meet customers in the small shuttered cottages on the fringe of town. I jump when my own rump is pinched by the one known as Rose May. She bats her eyelashes when I turn around.

For the next three hours I don't have time to even scratch an itch. I'm serving and cleaning up, steadily. With a day off coming to them, the men aren't so careful about how much they're drinking or how sloppy they're becoming. The fiddle music starts up in McIntyre's Hall down Dominion Avenue, and the sound of stomping feet and wild dancing spills into the street.

Once the bar closes, I go down to the laundry, where I find Violet in a cranky mood. She has three children with the chicken pox at home, and in the past twenty-four hours she's had less than thirty minutes of sleep. She whacks away at the sheets like she has it in for them—plunging and paddling them with all the strength in her porky arms. She says she isn't in much of a mood to talk, although every now and again she does say something that lets me know what's going through her mind. Mostly she seems to be considering how she's supposed to get everything done that needs doing. It's becoming too much and she's getting tuckered out, working at the hotel at night and tending her children during the day. When is she supposed to get her bread baked or her chores done? When is she supposed to get her sleep?

Each of these questions is followed with a good hearty whack at the sheets with the paddle.

Of course I have no answer when she glances up from the boiling pot looking for one, sweat gathering on her brow.

Sunday morning and it's quiet as a churchyard as I step onto the street. The smells and echoes of Saturday night still hang in the air. Only those tending animals are up and about. I take a turn to visit Cody at McDonald's Livery before I head to the eastern flats.

I grab a currycomb and spend a little time giving him a grooming. I know stabling him at a proper livery is an expense and luxury I can hardly afford. Few fellows who pitch a tent in the camp even own a horse, and those who do just let them graze freely, hobbling them at night. But those horses are mostly old hacks or screws, worthless to anyone but their owners, who depend on them to get about the territories as they look for work. West Coast Cody, on the other hand, is worth a lot, and I can't risk losing him. Once I finish brushing him, I take him for a ride along the wagon trail.

The cottages along Alberta Avenue are quiet—the miners get to spend a morning with their families. I stop to have a morning smoke with Francis Rochette, who asks how I'm getting on.

"Not too badly," I tell him. We lean against the wall of the stable, watching the sky turn from rose to pink. I consider the events that have occurred since he sent me off with the tarps. "Except for Mr. Ling Yu—the Chinaman who killed himself. That was a terrible affair."

"A Chinaman killed himself?"

I can't believe he hasn't heard. He isn't that far away from the campsite as the crow flies. "Yes," I say. "He couldn't stand the loneliness. You didn't hear?"

Francis draws on his smoke, lets a ring drift off into the sky and grinds the heel of his boot into the earth. "Charlie, most of us outside—we don't hear much of what goes on in the camp. The fact is, those fellows you're tenting with in the valley move about as often as the wind changes directions. They don't fit in with the town folk because most of the time they don't speak the language, and they like to stick to their own customs and ways. That doesn't usually sit well with those who are already established. Many prefer to pretend that those from a foreign land, and without a permanent home, don't really exist."

"How do they work together then? If they all talk different languages, how are they able to work side by side in the mine? Or on the railroad crews?"

Francis thinks about this. "Each man knows his own job. There's not much need for talking while they're working. Not if they know what they're doing, and many have worked in mines or on construction crews before they came to the West. Besides, the company bosses like it that way."

"Why?"

"Because if the fellows can't talk, they can't complain. They can't get together and bellyache about their poor wages and their dangerous work conditions. They can't discuss their pitiful housing or how they have to go into debt for all the extras like blankets and their own tools. If they can't get together on things, they won't discover they all feel mistreated. That way, they'll keep going on the way they are and they won't go on strike."

Francis seems to have those in charge of running things all figured out. I tell him I don't think it can go on like that forever; some day those fellows will have to talk.

I give him a hand feeding the pit horses. There are more than fifty, and every one is good-tempered and sure-footed. They have to be in order to work in the mine.

"You know, Charlie, you're awfully good with these horses," Francis tells me. "If you're trying to get work at the mine, you might suggest to Mr. Ash that you'd like to be a driver. Each horse has its own. You're responsible for his watering and grooming, as well as things like keeping his tack cleaned and oiled so he doesn't get harness sores. I'd be happy to recommend you."

I tell him I'd be grateful for that. I leave the mine livery, ride past Thornley's Shoe Shop and McVeigh's construction camp, where only a few men are camped. Off in the distance I can see Graham's Dairy Farm. Just past the farm, I know old Andy Grissack will be on his way to check his traps. The early morning mist is beginning to rise and burn off, so I turn and head back in the direction of Frank. Once Cody is stabled, I return to my camp to get some sleep.

It's around noon when I wake up. I have a new neighbor—he pitched a tent while I was sleeping. He's taken the space Mr. Ling Yu had occupied before he'd taken his life. Niko the Finn, he calls himself. Niko is about thirty years old and stocky, with a moustache the size of a boot brush. He probably spotted the open space and thought himself lucky to find a snug spot near both water and trees.

Twelve

Over the next two weeks there are two accidents at the mine. A fall of rock maims a pit pony at the same time as it breaks the collarbone of the driver. And a small gas explosion throws a boy of fourteen against a wall in the mine. He'd been working with his father in one of the chambers. The impact split his head and he fell forward, laid out cold.

I have just fallen asleep when I hear the father—accompanied by Evan Kostos, the big man in the sheepskin waistcoat—huffing and puffing into the campsite with the boy draped limply in his arms. It's the father's hollering and wailing that draws the attention of all of us in the camp. I lift the door I've fashioned in my tent. The boy's head lolls listlessly from side to side, and his long hair is matted with blood. It oozes from a large gash in his head.

Following close behind come others I recognize from the camp—Niko the Finn, and the Welshman, Tom Roberts. Both men still tote their handpicks. James is also with them, as are two others I only know by sight. They follow the father to his campsite, talking in their various languages. They still wear their mining caps, and their Wolf lamps swing from their belts. Their faces are entirely black with coal dust so that their teeth flash as white as buffalo bones when they speak.

The father lays his son on a blanket and sets about mopping his head with rags. I now realize the fellows are trying to talk him into allowing them to take the boy to Dr. Malcolmson in town. I move closer to follow what is going on.

"That wound's not going to heal without stitching," Evan is telling him. "Come on, now, father, let us take him in so the doctor can sew it up right."

"Evan's right," Niko the Finn agrees. "The boy's already lost a kettlefull of blood. If the doctor don't stop it, he's going to bleed dry."

The two men gently try to pry the troubled father, Mr. Bruce Stewart, away from the boy. I don't understand why Mr. Stewart continues to cling to his lad, why he is so reluctant to give him up. He has to know the men are right about him needing a doctor's attention.

"Go away, all of you. I can look after my own child." Mr. Stewart presses the rag hard to his son's head. Blood quickly soaks through. He wipes his own face, smearing the coal dust with blood. "I've been through some tough knocks myself, and I've seen much worse than this. Why, in Sydney, we saved a fellow who'd lost his arm, cut clean off. Lost twice this much blood just coming up in the cage. My boy Douglas here is as tough as nails, comes from a long line of the same. If you want to be helpful—someone get me another rag."

Another fellow in the camp has already run for some sturdy strips of sackcloth, which he passes to Evan Kostos. Mr. Stewart leans back long enough to allow Evan to bind Douglas's head tight, closing the gash the best he can. As he does, I overhear him tell the father that if it's the doctor's bill he's worried about, they'll find a way. If the mine charges him, it doesn't have to be paid all at once. He can arrange to have it deducted over time.

Mr. Stewart sighs heavily. He wipes his nose on his bloody cuff and collapses back onto the grass. Evan Kostos's words seem to have pierced something in him. In dribbles and drabs, all his troubles then begin to leak out. "Me and my boy—we've been here not two weeks and it cost everything we had just to come out. I've got a wife and five more at home in Cape Breton counting on what we send. Douglas has been working alongside me since he was a boy. He started as a breaker, then came down in the pit as a trapper until he proved himself. We had to give it up there, though. The pit closes in winter, along with the ports. A fellow can't make enough for a family to live on by only working part of the year. Until we can afford to move up to posher surroundings, we've been camping here where it doesn't cost us. But we won't be moving anywhere if we start running up doctor's bills."

"Yes, I know," Tom Roberts tells him. "Most of us here are sending money back, feeding families of our own."

Mr. Stewart's eyes flash up to Tom Roberts—suddenly hopeful. Like he's caught sight of a single friendly face across a room of sour ones. "I've got two more boys who'll be ready for the pit soon enough. They're nine and eleven, and as soon as they can read and write, they'll be ready to go. They can't wait to get down below with their dad and big brother. They talk about it all the time. When that day comes, oh boy, then we'll be making some money."

While they talk, Evan Kostos and Niko the Finn take the opportunity to roll the sides of the blanket Douglas lies in like it's a hammock. The boy's eyes are now open, although they stare blankly at the sky. Lifting the ends, the men hoist him into the air. They are joined by other fellows who grab the sides to help carry Douglas into town. James offers his hand to Mr. Stewart and pulls him to his feet. The two of them follow behind the procession as they cross the flats toward Gold Creek.

Once they are out of hearing range, Tom Roberts pulls off his hat, flipping it so the peak hangs down. "All right, boys, who'll chip in? I'm taking up a collection for the boy's doctoring bill. Whatever you can give, I'll accept. We've all got to eat, but Mr. Bruce Stewart's got five at home, as well as the injured one here. I expect if any of us were in a similar position, he'd be doing the same for us. Whatever you can afford, fellows. It means six children eating or starving to him, and to you—only a few less minutes spent at the bar."

Tom Roberts walks among those gathered. It's most likely that many can't even understand the meaning of his words, yet there isn't any hesitation from the men. Everyone who's standing digs in his pockets and produces something. Those of us who can understand know he is right. It could very well be one of us who's the next to suffer unfortunate circumstances. Then there are the blood splatters at our feet and, although nobody says a word about it, the remembrance of Ling Yu. I guess that giving makes us all feel a little less guilty and a little less lonesome somehow.

I return to my tent. When I wake up, Douglas is already back at the camp. He's needed nine stitches to close up the gash. Within a few hours he is strutting about, brandishing his bandage like a shiny medal received for his efforts in the mine.

"Do you think he'll go back in the mine?" I ask James once he's returned from work. We're having a smoke, jabbering while our suppers cook, something we've become accustomed to doing.

"Go back in the mine? Of course he will. He wanted to go back tomorrow, but the doctor's insisting he stay put. He's a scrappy lad, Douglas is, already pit-hardened. They start working in the mines at a younger age in the East. At fourteen he's ahead of most of the boys his age who work at the picking table, sorting and pulling out waste. They dream of going down in the pit and he's already down there. He's a foul-mouthed rascal too." James laughs. "Already chewing plug, drinking whiskey and swearing as skillfully as the older chaps. But it's in his breeding. He comes from a place where mining is what the folks do. Me, I'm going to make my money and get out of here. I'm going to live my life on top of the earth, where the sun shines and there's no danger of getting your lungs clogged up with soot."

James and I visit Douglas, taking what we have on hand to build his strength: a jug of fresh milk and sweet cakes. The cakes are four days old and a little dried out, but I wasn't going to turn them down when they were offered to me by Sam at the hotel. We ask if there's anything we can do to help ease his pain.

But Douglas, the cocky rogue that he is, swears he doesn't feel any pain. He's feeling just as fit as any of us sorry bastards, and if he needs any mothering he sure won't be calling on us. He'll be finding his comfort in the arms of Rose May.

He's had a mighty knock on the gourd. I'm quite certain he must have been overcome with a fit of delirium to be talking to us like that, but James is standing next to me trying not to laugh.

"What'd I tell you?" he says on the way back to our tents. "Scrappier than a cock before he's let loose in the ring. Always gearing up for a fight."

"What makes him that way?"

James shrugs. "I don't know that he really is."

Douglas doesn't seem to mind our company, despite us being sorry bastards. He wanders over to my tent after supper to join James and me for a cup of tea. He pulls a flask from his pocket and stirs a fine wallop of whiskey into it, careful to make sure both James and I take notice of it.

"That's probably not the best thing for an already aching head," James tells him. "At least, not once the effects have worn off."

Douglas spits on the ground. "Then I won't let it wear

off. I can always get my hands on another pint. I've been drinking it since I was ten years old."

"Ten?" inquires James.

"My older brother used to get it for me."

James glances at me. "Where's your brother now?"

Douglas takes a long haul on the cup before answering. "That brother's dead. Killed when a support timber gave out and a section of roof caved in. It happened almost two years ago. Victor and two other men killed along with him. He was six months older than I am right now."

"You must miss him," says James.

"Naw." Douglas shakes his head. "Well, I guess I do, sometimes. But I got so many others. Soon they'll all be down in the pit."

Douglas doesn't say any more about his brother. Instead, he tells us how he'd been a trapper at Sydney and become quite an expert at drowning rats. He had to find a way to pass the time as he waited to open ventilation doors for the horses and tubs to pass through.

"It starts to drive you crazy when all you can hear— besides the echoes of the picks and the blasted tubs rumbling and the water dripping—are those rats. They skitter around you, sometimes so close you can feel their whiskers across your skin. But you can't see them, except once in a while when you catch one scurrying by in the beam of your light. So I made trails with broken-off bits of bread. I made them lead across to a bucket filled with water. When I heard a plop, I knew I'd got one and I'd slap a lid over it, quick as I could. He'd thrash around in there for a minute or so until he stopped and I could only hear the other rumbling sounds again. Then I'd hear another skitter close by. I'd fish the drowned one out by the tail and toss him in a corner. Some days I'd catch as many as ten. But there was no end to them."

James throws his last dregs of tea in the fire. "When are you going back into the mine?"

"My dad wants me to go down tomorrow—he's afraid they'll fill my position if I don't. But the doctor won't have me go back for a few days. Not until my head's done some healing."

"You'd be best to take the doctor's advice," says James.

Mr. Stewart relents and allows Douglas to stay in camp and rest over the next two days. But on the third day he expects him to return. If he doesn't, he is certain they will replace him with one of the many fellows begging for work.

It's quiet that evening at the Imperial Hotel. Only one or two squabbles break out over gambling debts. Violet Love is looking worse off than I've seen her all week. Four of her five children now have the chicken pox. Between caring for them and her husband, she's had very little sleep. I take over the heavy work, pounding and paddling the sheets while she does the hanging and pressing. My own arms are beginning to look as rosy and raw as Violet's.

The sun isn't up as I head onto Dominion, but I can already feel the beginnings of a very warm day. Mr. Steeves is giving me a couple of days off—the first I've had since I started working for him—so I'm looking forward to that.

The long blast of a train whistle tells me the Spokane Flyer is leaving town. Miners are filing toward Turtle Mountain, the milk and coal wagons are making their deliveries, and people are beginning to drift into town. By the time I pass the miners' shacks, the darker shades of early morning are lifting to gray. I look to see which of my neighbors have changed. There are always a few who have given up trying to find work and moved on. And then there are others who, after hearing of opportunities in Frank, have just arrived.

Lamps glow from within the makeshift tents. Close enough now, I suddenly realize there's a dim light within my own! I stand outside, listening to who, or what, is rustling around inside. I jump when a figure passes before the lamp and a giant, distorted shadow with a monstrous head falls across the wall of the tarp. It has to be a grizzly bear. I recall stories of how other fellows had lost everything when their camp was raided by a bear. I'm about to run to James for a weapon when I realize it isn't like an animal to use the door. Not without mincing it to shreds.

I push the canvas aside. It's Douglas, with his big bandaged head, going through my belongings. He's picking through things carefully so as not to disturb them too much.

I always carry my money with me. Some desperate people travel through the territories, and many of those wouldn't consider it thievery to help themselves to what's left lying around in an empty tent. So I hadn't left anything worth lifting. Still, I can see Douglas has claimed something, which is tucked in the waist of his trousers and shows as a bulge beneath his shirt. I wait until he's turned his back before I plunge inside and rush him. It's a delicate thing, rushing the wounded. It has to be done carefully so I don't break open his stitches and start him gushing all over again.

It doesn't take much effort to grab him from behind and put him in a headlock. "What are you doing in my tent? Took a wrong turn, did you? Thought you may as well pinch a few things since you're here?" I tighten my hold.

Douglas puts up a struggle. But he's a couple of years younger than me and not at his strongest after being whomped on the head. He grapples at my arms, clinched around his neck. "Let go. I wasn't doing anything. I was only looking."

"Oh, yeah. What's in your trousers?"

Douglas's one hand flies from his neck to grasp whatever is beneath his shirt. He continues to struggle with the other arm while keeping hold of the bulge so it doesn't slip out.

I pull tighter. "What'd you lift? Show me."

"Let go of me, Charlie, you're choking me. And my head hurts."

"Oh, so now it hurts, does it? Come on, now. Let me see what you're hiding."

"Okay, but only if you let me go."

I release my hold. He backs up. The flame in the lamp flickers, causing our shadows to wobble across the tarp. I stand in front of the flap to block his escape in case he decides to bolt. "What is it?"

Douglas sighs and pulls *The Pilgrim's Progress* from his shirt. He holds the dog-eared book toward me.

I stare at it a moment, wondering why he'd pinch something so common. He most certainly wouldn't get much money for it, if anyone was inclined to buy it at all. I take it from him. "What were you going to do with this?"

"Read it."

If he had no intention of selling it, of course it would make sense that he'd read it. Still, reading doesn't seem like something a pit-hardened, whiskey-swilling lad would do. "Why?"

He shrugs. "To see if I can still read."

"What do you mean—still? You can read?" I wasn't meaning to make fun of him, but not many I'd met in the territories could.

Douglas has trouble looking me in the eye. "Charlie," he says in a changed voice—a smaller, more cautious voice. It might even have drawn some pity from me if I hadn't caught him skulking around my tent. "I can't go back into the mine. I'm scared. I don't want to end up like Victor. I hate the cold and the wet and the dust that's always making it hard to breathe. I hate the noises. You can't ever be sure what you're hearing. I'm terrified of the dark."

"What do you want to do then?"

But he doesn't have a ready answer. He shrugs. "All I know is I was good at school. The teacher in the seventh form said I had the intelligence to do anything. She said I didn't have to go down in the pit if I didn't want."

"So why did you? Why didn't you keep going to school?"

In a gesture of frustration, he throws his hands in the air. "Where I come from, that just isn't the way it works. You can't *decide* to keep going to school just because you want to or a teacher tells you you're smart. You go down in the pit because your dad does and that's what your dad's always done. And his dad too. And Victor. And so my brothers will too. They're all so eager to get out of school and go down. But not me."

"Maybe you should talk to your dad. Maybe, if you really want to do something different, he'll understand."

Douglas groans. "There's no reason or sense in doing that. It won't be talking, it'll be listening to him. Mining life was good enough for all who came before me, and if it was good enough for him and his father, it's good enough for me too. It's what puts bread and butter on our table."

"Well, it seems to me if you really don't like it, you shouldn't have to spend your whole life at it."

"Charlie, have you ever wanted to fly?" Douglas is now looking straight at me. He says it almost breathlessly, like the words have been waiting to soar out. "That's what I want to do more than anything else. I want to be an airman and operate a flying machine. I read all about it in some books I took out of the lending library. They were full of descriptions and drawings of gliders and other flying machines. One of the books was called *On Aerial Navigation*. The ideas are nearly a hundred years old, but Mr. George Cayley, who wrote it, had figured out that fixed wings, a power system for propulsion and a tail for control are what an aeroplane needs to fly. It's already been done in America. Mr. Langley's aerodrome used a steam engine for propulsion. It was too heavy to take a pilot, but it's being worked on and it won't be long. There are two fellows in America right now—they run a bicycle shop and they've got the design of the wings just right. It's the power source they've got to work on, but maybe in the next year…"

All the while he's talking, Douglas's eyes are growing brighter and his face is getting more flushed. Suddenly he seems to realize he's getting carried away with his answer and he breaks off.

"Well, anyway, that's what I want to do. I want to fly. I hate being underground. It's dark and it smells old and musty, and the work is wearisome." Douglas sighs. "I'd better go make the old man something to eat before he starts hollering. He's been doing the work of both of us the past couple of days and he's snappier than a pit dog."

I step aside, allowing Douglas to leave the tent. I look at the book in my hand. "Here," I say, offering it to him. "Go ahead and take it. I haven't much use for it."

"You don't mind me borrowing it? You don't have to give it to me. I just want to try reading it. Just to see."

I shake my head. "No, you keep it, although there's nothing in it about flying machines. But I've probably read it a hundred times. It's time I got something different."

Douglas accepts the book and leaves my tent.

Thirteen

I'm awake just before noon. The sun is beating down, making it like a steam bath inside the canvas, and my clothes are clamped to my skin with sweat. Even the tarp is sweating.

I toss about a bit. I even try blocking the light by covering my face with a flannel, but that only gets me hotter, and I'm struck by a terrific fear that I might suffocate if I fall asleep like that. Finally I get up, light the fire and make coffee. I then do some laundering of my own before heading into town for more supplies.

I pick up a bit of bacon at Pat Burns' Meat Market before heading over to the bakery. I've just left the shop when I spot Rose May ahead of me with her arm around the waist of a younger girl. I'm looking from the back, but I can't shake the feeling that I've seen her before. I walk quicker. I'm no more than fifteen feet away when the wind catches the hem of her skirt, revealing the moccasins on her feet.

"Maddie!"

She turns. But instead of acknowledging me, she faces forward again.

"Maddie, don't you remember me?" I cut in front of the two of them. "It's Charlie."

Maddie drops her head so that I can no longer see her eyes. They are hidden beneath the brim of her bonnet. I wonder if she's avoiding me because of Willie Many Horses and what he does. Perhaps I should tell her that I know as well as anyone that even the most honest fellow may feel forced to do something he normally wouldn't do to save his hide. But there's no point in going into all that until I know for sure why she's avoiding me.

Rose May stops walking. She faces me, cocking an eyebrow in an inquisitive way. "Charlie, how is it that you know Maddie?"

"I stayed with her family in their camp, back near Pincher Creek."

"Well, I don't know where that family is now, but she's coming to live with me. Look at her—the poor girl is starving to death. I found her on the street this morning nearly collapsed, she's so exhausted and in need of food. She's agreed to help mind our establishment, to do the chores and run errands for my girls in exchange for food and a roof over her head."

I look at Maddie more closely. Rose May is right. Maddie looks thin as a cat, squashed the way she is against Rose May's fleshy self. Her face is much thinner than I recall, and the pitiful clothes she wears make her look like she's been fed through a mangle. I wonder what happened to her buckskin dress with all its fancy quilling.

Rose May smiles and pinches Maddie's wasted cheek. "If we can get her fattened up, we might even get the fellows interested. I expect Maddie here will be a fair charmer with a little added weight. What do you think, Charlie?"

It takes me a second to take in her meaning, but when I do, I look at her in horror. I don't answer, but grab Maddie and wrench her free of Rose May's arm. I pull her with me, stumbling at my heels—my only thought being to get her as far away from Rose May as I can. Rose May screeches and hollers behind us, throwing her chubby fists in the air. I glance back. She's making a lot of noise, but she isn't following. I duck around to the back door of the Imperial Hotel, where I lead Maddie into the empty laundering room. We are both pulling hard to get air into our lungs when I finally speak.

"You're not going with her," I say. I'm afraid of Maddie running off, so I continue to hold tight to her arm. "What are you doing here? Where's the rest of your family?"

Maddie folds forward a little before she starts to cry. Her legs seem to give up entirely. "Charlie, let go, you're hurting me. I'm not going to run. I have no place to run to."

I let go of her wrist, but I catch her in my arms as she slowly crumples to the floor. I let her go on and cry for a while—it might help lighten her troubles if she does. Finally she dabs at her eyes with the ragged ends of her cloak. "Father's in jail because he wouldn't let them put Henry and me in school. Even after they found us, he tried to prevent it."

"Is that where you've been? Is that why you're dressed this way?"

She nods. "It's where I'm running away from. I left a week ago, after they sent Henry home. They sent him back to the reserve because he's come down with tuberculosis. He's sicker than I've ever seen him. They said there was nothing more they could do. The baby's near ready to die, and Mother's sick too. I want to be with them, but she won't let me because I'm well. She won't have me come down with it too. Besides, she's too worn and tired to put up with any more trouble from the school. I'm not her responsibility anymore, she told me. Only the school can tell me what to do. They had to sign to it. It's a terrible place, Charlie." Maddie begins to cry again.

Not knowing what else to do, I pull her head against my shoulder.

"They took away our clothes and gave us these awful things to wear. They feed us barely enough to keep us standing on our feet. They burned all the boys' medicine bags. They put them in the stove and set them on fire. They cut their hair off too. They thrash us if we speak anything but English. They're trying to thrash all the Indian out of us. They say our families and our way of life is shameful and heathenly, and it's their duty to make us civilized."

I don't know what to say. Then I remember my bread and cheese. Maddie tries to be ladylike about accepting it, but she's so hungry, she tears into it with little insistence from me.

"How'd you wind up in Frank?"

She answers between mouthfuls. "I hid in a wagon. I knew it was leaving the school, going into Pincher Creek for supplies. All night I waited, crouched in the box beneath the tarp. Just before we reached town, I jumped off. I hid in a farmer's hayloft until I ran out of the food I'd snuck from the school pantry. I was just about fainting from hunger, so this morning I climbed in his hay wagon after he'd hitched it up. This is where it stopped." Maddie trembles as she draws in a long breath. "Charlie, I don't know where to go or what to do. I can't go back to that place. I can't go home or I'll get sick, like so many others."

"No, you can't," I agree.

Maddie is all plugged up with tears and having trouble swallowing. I fill a glass of water from the pump and hand it to her. I'm not sure what to do either. I can't take her back to my camp in the valley, not with all those fellows and no women around. I think of Violet Love. "Maddie, can you wait here for me? Just for ten minutes. Don't worry, I don't expect anyone will come in. I work here and we do the laundry at night. Hide in that storage room. It's got a window and you'll be safe. I'm going to talk to someone who might be able to help us."

Maddie nods. She quickly finishes her drink. I see that she's comfortable enough in the storage closet with a stack of clean towels to sit on. I then make her promise again that she'll wait for me, and I go off to find Violet Love. I don't know who else I can trust.

Violet lives in one of the miners' cottages at the end of Dominion Avenue, behind the boarding house. She'd pointed it out to me one morning, although even if she hadn't, I don't know that I'd need directions. I can hear her voice through an open window as I come down the street. I know her temper is just about stretched to snapping, what with her sick children and her lack of sleep. I turn into her yard, where I step over a broken china doll and knock on the front door. Violet is surprised to see me, of course.

"Charlie, well, I don't ever see you in daylight. Come on in and have a dish of porridge with us." She motions me through the door with a big wooden spoon.

But I stand where I am, not wanting to intrude, especially after spotting the tots behind her. Their small hands wipe at runny noses, and they madly scratch at their skin. Two older ones sitting at a table clamour for the porridge she's been stirring on the stove.

"I appreciate you asking, but no, thank you. I really don't want to take much of your time." I then quickly explain my visit. When I finish, I wait for Violet to tell me what's on her mind. I haven't asked her for anything specific. I've told her that I most importantly want her advice. But I do tell her I can't let Maddie end up in Rose May's sporting house. I don't know how she's going to react to Maddie being an Indian. You think you know someone, but you can never really be sure how a person is made until you're faced with something like this.

I know I've been a good judge of her when she slaps her hands on her hip.

"Well, what did you go leave her sitting in a closet for?" She pierces the air with the wooden spoon. "Go get her, you donkey's duff. Maybe now I can get a bit of rest while she minds my brood. If she doesn't mind plain cooking and sharing sleeping quarters with the little ones, I can gladly feed her until she's found a place to go."

I jump from the stoop and take off down the street to rescue Maddie from the closet where I'd left her holed up.

It's early evening when I return from getting Maddie settled. Mr. Bruce Stewart's booming voice echoes throughout the camp. He's hollering if anyone has seen Douglas—not asking anyone in particular as he paces around the tents. I look up from where I'm poking at my fire when he nears James and me.

"Have you seen my Douglas? I haven't seen hide nor hair of him since I left this morning. No supper waiting or heated water ready for his father to have a wash. The boy gets a crack on the head and he's no good for anything. I told him his holiday was over. Tomorrow he's going back to work. If you see him, tell him his father's looking for him. You might also warn him to watch out for his hide. Idleness doesn't run in this family."

"Yes, sir," James answers from where he's frying his supper. He moves his coffee pot to the grate.

I nod so that Mr. Stewart will know that I've heard what he said. As soon as he moves on, James waves me over to his camp. When I get there, he motions me into his tent. "Charlie, come in here," he says in an odd way.

I follow him in.

"Someone was in here. They helped themselves to a few of my things."

I glance around at the small stove he's installed to heat the place, his bedroll, and the wooden crates where he stores his food. He also owns a small rough-built table. "How can you tell? I can't see that it looks disturbed."

"I know it doesn't. I didn't realize it myself until I started looking. But I left my hatchet over there by the stove, and my storage crates have been rummaged through. It's mostly food that's missing, and nothing's been vandalized. Oh, and I had a couple of books on the shelf there, by my head. They're gone, but whoever it was left my pocket watch. It was sitting next to the books, right out in the open. It's not worth much, but it was given to me at one of my foster homes. Now why would he take food and books and leave what little was valuable?"

I shrug. "I guess he wasn't taking just for the sake of having. He only took what he thought he needed to survive."

James looks at me.

"Douglas hated mining. He never wanted to do it; you were right about him. Anyway, I think we ought to give him time to put some distance between him and his dad."

"But if he doesn't show up tomorrow, his position will be gone. What if he changes his mind?"

"I don't think he will. He was awfully determined."

"Charlie." James pauses before touching his forehead. It's something I've seen him do in the past, most usually when an idea is forming. But a moment later he says, "Never mind."

I am splitting kindling when he wanders over to my camp a half hour later. "I've been thinking; you've got another day off, why don't you take Douglas's place? It will buy him at least one more day. You may be right; he may be gone for good, but just in case."

I'm quite certain Douglas won't be back and it will serve no purpose. But for my own sake, it would give me a chance to try out work in the mine.

James is able to convince Mr. Stewart of his plan. He doesn't tell him we know Douglas ran off—just that it might help hold his job. The next morning I head up Dominion alongside the other miners. Douglas's identification tag is tucked in my pocket. Once I've collected my Wolf lamp, I hang the tag on the miners' checkboard in the lamphouse. James explains how the lamp man checks the board at the end of a shift. If there are any tags left hanging, he knows a fellow is still in the mine and could be in trouble.

We enter the mine through the lamphouse—I follow James into the pitch by way of a crude flight of stairs. The main gangway is shored up with timbers at the angle the coal seams run, and I feel like I'm trying to keep my footing in the hold of a listing ship. Water drips around us and the smell of sulfur drifts from a nearby spring. The clink and thud of picks loosening coal is drowned out by the noise from an approaching train of cars. The clatter becomes deafening—there are seven of them in all, hauled by a single draft horse. It's nearing the main portal and moving at a mighty good clip. Down the line, the spragger stands ready to brake it. As we start down the tunnel, I don't take my eyes from James's lamp ahead of me—that and the sound of his voice seem the only things to be real.

With everything propped up by timbers, it seems we are walking through a dark forest of gnarled trees. But there are no earthly sounds of the wind or birds or animals, only the mechanical noises of men working the seams and moving buckets—dumping coal into carts. We walk a long way, miles it seems, into the belly of the mountain.

I'm working on the dusting team with James and three other men. Our team foreman is a man by the name of Mr. Amos Barr. Our job is to sprinkle calcium flour over the dug-out areas to keep the coal dust down and the invisible gases like methane from building up. We haul the large bags of calcium along with us in a metal cart to the mined-out rooms where pillars of coal have been left to support the roof.

"Eventually they'll take those out too," James tells me, "and this room will be left to collapse."

We are quickly covered in the white powder. The men I work with are like ghosts moving about the black mine. The powder burns my eyes and nose and scorches my lungs. The strangeness of where I am forces me to stay alert. Still, by mid-morning I've cracked my head more than once and grazed my shoulder, tearing my shirt.

I am working with my head down when I hear a sudden close clatter and James cries, "Charlie!" from across the space. At the same time, Amos grabs hold of my collar and wrenches me back. A breath of wind, and a resounding crash shakes the rock next to me. I turn. If not for Amos plucking me out of the way, I would have been crushed against the wall by the runaway dusting cart. It got away from one of the men. Amos takes a minute to lecture *me*—not the fellow responsible. "If you want to be sitting down to dinner tonight, lad, you've got to have eyes in the back of your head. You need ears sharp as a hawk's and a nose like a bloodhound's. And even those things will only give you an advantage. Many fellows have had them all and still wound up dead."

I answer him with a solemn nod.

Following Amos's directions, we work outward toward the main portal. I'm hauling another sack of dust from the cart when a crack like thunder shakes the mine. I think I've missed a step. I step backward into air and fall hard to the floor. While I am struggling to get up, Amos has already started toward the sound.

"It's a normal thing," James tells me. "The floors move when pressure is released in the chambers below."

James is trying to sound calm, but I detect there isn't a lot of conviction in his voice. Especially when the timber posts around us creak, and one or two begin to bow. Chunks of rock hurtle into the main tunnel. Men are now hollering, and the flood of lights in the gangway tells us it might be more serious than James thought. I follow him into the tunnel, where we are met by plumes of black smoke.

The head foreman quickly determines a nearby raise—a tunnel to the surface—has collapsed. He does a quick headcount. Niko and another miner by the name of Mikel are not among us. The miners immediately start digging into the collapsed vein.

Only so many can work in the confined space, so James and I pitch in by hauling away the coal and rubble they excavate. I heft bucket after bucket of rock into one of the large tubs. The men around me are breathing hard, sweating—rivulets of coal dust run from their brows, but no one complains. No one discusses the two men unaccounted for and the possibility they are lying broken beneath the collapsed rock. It strikes me that another collapse might be building or that this one could unleash some other disaster. If anyone else has the same thought, it doesn't distract them from their work.

While we work, the head foreman communicates to those outside by way of a system of bells strung through the mine.

"They broke through!" he suddenly shouts. "Our boys are on the surface."

As the news makes its way down the tunnel, the miners drop their picks and wipe their brows. They cough and spit to clear their lungs, recover their breath and discuss the collapse. After consulting with the other supervisors, the foreman determines the collapse was the result of a bump and tells us to return to our work. All around me, fellows start toward their stations. I am shaking—I don't know how I can go back to work. Others chat about what's happened or whatever else is on their minds. But I'm watching Niko, who has now returned and stopped to talk with the knot of men still clearing the collapsed vein—laughing—his white teeth shining through the soot.

"Come on, let's get moving," Amos tells me.

"The Indians wouldn't camp in the valley," James says as we return to where we'd been working. "Where we have our tents pitched, or where old Frank is sitting, either. They wouldn't camp anywhere near the foot of Turtle Mountain. They still won't. They say that it moves."

"How can a mountain move?"

He shrugs. "Johnson, one of the Indians who works for Mr. Graham, says the story comes down from his ancestors. The Indians used to mine chert, a stone they used to fashion their tools. I guess the old-timers were scared off by the way the mountain shuddered when they were inside it, the way it just did. They called Turtle Mountain the mountain that walks."

James breaks open another bag of calcium dust. The sounds of picks and carts clattering down the track have already resumed. "You know, Charlie, between you and me, I'm glad this is only for a couple of months. I'd much rather spend my time worrying about whether there's going to be enough rain to grow anything than if I'll be alive at the end of the day."

Fourteen

"**W**hy don't you come with me?" James asks me later that evening. "To my homestead. We'll break land a lot faster if there're two of us. Obviously I can't pay you in the beginning, but I can provide you with a place to live, and food. If we share duties, put together everything we know, it will surely be successful. And it wouldn't be nearly so lonely. You and me, Charlie, we think the same."

We are walking back to camp after exercising Cody. It's dark, and despite a good scrubbing down in the wash house, calcium dust still shimmers in James's hair.

It's a mighty tempting offer and I think about it, but if I work for James, I won't be able to save for my own land. "I appreciate the offer," I tell him, "but I've got to save money to get my own place. I don't want to be in debt to anyone again. I learned that from living with the Brooks."

I can hardly believe I've said it out loud. This is what I've been turning over in my mind since speaking with the McKays. But James is the first I've had the nerve to voice my ambitions to.

He frowns a little but quickly brightens again. "You could purchase close to me and we could help each other out. It would be as good as having kin close at hand."

"Yes, it would. I think that is a brilliant plan."

We are making our way through the camp when we are drawn to a conversation around Tom Roberts's fire. Most of the fellows who work in the mine, as well as camp in the valley, are gathered around. They sit on overturned buckets and drums, sip tea from tin cups, chew tobacco or pull on pipes in the hot blaze of the fire. Tom has a roaring one going—the weather has taken a turn and it's cooling off. It isn't a merry conversation; the men are discussing conditions in the mine. Tom Roberts kindly offers James and me cigarettes he's already rolled.

"We've been feeling tremors more and more frequently," he says to all those gathered. As he lights our smokes, the concern on his face shows in the flare of the match. "I'm told it's nothing new and they've always been there. Still, when you've got thousands of feet of rock over your head, you don't like to think that mountain's going to take a mind to shift."

"I've only been working there two weeks," says Evan Kostos, "but Mr. Chestnut says the tremors have been building over the past seven months. I myself can attest to the fact that coal falls without much encouragement. I've never come across anything quite like it in all my years in a pit."

"I hear men have left because of it," adds Tom. "Scared the pants off them when they felt it move and they wouldn't go back."

I turn to the fire while pondering what Violet Love had told me. How she was glad her husband, Peter, was on the picking table and out of the pit.

Mr. Bruce Stewart stands up. Drawing his pipe from his mouth, he moves next to the fire. "I'm not sure what you fellows are getting all worked up about. I've been working the pit since I was a boy of ten. There're natural movements, we all know that. The manager says it's in first-rate condition; the walls and roof are kept shored and solid, and there's nothing different here in Frank than there is in any other coal mine in this stretch of the Crow's Nest Pass."

Niko the Finn spits on the ground. "Well, Mr. Stewart, I'm inclined to disagree. Joe Chapman, foreman on the night crew, agrees they're occurring more often and they're concerning him. Says it's mostly between one and three in the morning. He likens it to a ship shuddering when it hits a big wave. I don't know, but that don't sound all that natural to me. There's got to be some reason the timbermen's work is splintered and twisted like twigs less than twelve hours after they've been put in."

"Well, we all need the jobs," says Evan. "Nobody can deny that. And we can't be put off by the accidents and what happened today. Let's all here tonight agree to keep our eyes and ears open. We know what we've heard and what we've been told. Let's talk again in a few weeks and determine then if the situation has changed."

The fellows agree it's about all that can be done. James and I finish our smokes. He stays on to talk, but I turn in. I'm chilled to the bone and could kick myself again for leaving my mackinaw at the stopping house.

I lie awake for some time, thinking about the conversation and the collapse of the raise. I begin to wonder if working in the mine is a wise decision. But I don't know of any other job where I'll be able to make wages of up to three dollars a day. Besides, if it's true what James said—that the Indian miners were complaining about the tremors thousands of years ago—then miners will still be complaining about them in a thousand more.

Maddie is getting on well looking after Violet Love's children. She says they've settled down since the worst of their sickness is over. "Course it also helps that Mr. and Mrs. Love have got some sleep." She laughs a little. "They're not making their miserable children even more miserable by minding them when their own nerves are frayed."

Maddie has also calmed down with some food in her and a decent place to sleep, although she is still very worried about her mother, Little Crow and the baby. She has no way of getting news. But she has received a speck of hope—Peter Love works with a fellow who is acquainted with a man by the name of Father Albert Lacombe. Maddie tells me the Indians know him as Ars-Okitsiparpi, "the man of the good heart." He's helped many Indians in the northwest with their troubles, and Peter's friend hopes he can interest him in helping Maddie's dad.

She's telling me all this as we stroll down Dominion Avenue late in the afternoon. It's turned bitterly cold, and Maddie pulls the thin shawl she wears tighter about her shoulders.

"Mr. Love's friend is going to see if he can get word of my mother and brothers. They've been awfully kind to me, Charlie, and it's all thanks to you."

I'm about to deny this when a familiar voice comes bellowing from behind me. "Charlie Sutherland!"

It instantly causes me to cringe. I don't want to believe it, but it's true. When I turn around, there stands Buck Brooks, leaning up against the Imperial Hotel, just watching traffic pass by.

"Well, now, ain't it a twist of fate that I'd come across you here." Buck shakes his burly head, straightens and spits a wad of tobacco juice on the boardwalk at his feet. Duke, the dapple gray, stands at the hitching post.

Of course I want to run, but I stay put. Not that it has anything to do with me being courageous; it has everything to do with being frozen to that spot with fear. "I don't believe it is a twist of fate. I believe you found I was in Frank by asking around."

By the way he is gaping, I can see that Buck Brooks is shocked at my being so bold. What he doesn't know is that I've shocked myself even more.

"Well, listen to you. Haven't you got some lip in the past month." He looks at Maddie. "And cavorting with the savages too. I should expect you'd be drawn to your own kind.

But I suppose I have to give you credit for being right. Funny thing is, I've been asking around and nobody in this town has run into a no-good, deceitful Home boy."

"Buck, I'm telling you flat out—I had nothing to do with Albert's death. My guess is he was so filled with liquor he got turned around and couldn't find his way back to the house. You know he was capable, and that's what he did. I'm sorry I slept through it. It was a terrible thing and I wouldn't have wished it even on someone as mean-spirited as him."

Buck only nods before taking another step forward. "Well, I'm glad you can find some sympathy for Albert in your heart. But I haven't come to bring you up on a charge of murder. As it turns out, the Mounted Police see no cause. They seem to be in agreement with you when it comes to how Albert met his end. What I've come for is simply to collect what's due. That would be the work you still owe me for taking you in and keeping you sheltered and fed for coming up three years. The snow's about gone from the fields and they're nearly ready to start tilling, and you, Charlie Sutherland, have got a legal contract to fulfill."

Maddie steps forward. "Mr. Brooks—"

But that's as far as she gets because I grab her arm and tug her back. I pull her close to me. I don't trust what Buck might say or do to her any more than I'd trust the response of a rabid dog.

To my surprise, he waves us on. "That's all right now, you and your Indian go about your business. It's too late to leave tonight. It's nearly dark, it's cloudy and cold enough it might snow. We'll start out first thing in the morning. I'm staying right here at the Imperial Hotel. Nobody seemed to know the Home boy I was describing, but they did say a young fellow by the name of Charlie worked here. He'd be back working tonight. Just be sure when you return you bring your belongings. We'll start out at first light."

Buck follows what he says with one of his grins. It's as spiteful as I remember it to be. My mind and heart are racing as I take Maddie's hand, and she hurries along next to me.

"Charlie, what are you going to do? Maybe you should talk to Constable Leard."

"I can't."

"Why can't you?"

"I can't because Buck is right about one thing: by the contract of the Home, I have to go back. You go back to Violet Love's cottage now. I've got to figure this out my own way. Don't worry, Maddie, I'm not going anywhere. I can't. I have a decent job and I have friends in the camp and nowhere else to go."

Maddie is reluctant, but she kisses my forehead before heading back to the Loves' cottage by a different route.

Francis Rochette is working outside the mine livery, currying a horse, when I turn off the wagon trail headed toward the camp. "Charlie," he calls.

I've been lost in my pondering. I look up and see him wave.

"There was a fellow looking for you." He continues brushing the horse as I approach. "A couple of hours ago. A big hairy fellow on a gray shire. He said he was your uncle, although I can't say he looked or talked even a bit like you. But he did say you'd be surprised to see him because it had been such a long time. Anyway, I gave him directions to your camp. Did you meet up with him?"

There is no point getting angry with Francis. He couldn't have known who he was directing. "Yes," I say. "I ran into him in town."

I turn and head back toward my tent. At the same time I hear Francis stop brushing the horse. "Are you all right, Charlie?"

I lift a hand to let him know that I am.

"No, I mean in your camp. Are you warm enough? It's dreadfully cold today. It's got to be colder than any day this past winter. Nearly May, and I'll be breaking ice for the horses in the morning."

He must have seen me shivering despite the three shirts I'm wearing. "I'm fine. I'm indoors all night, and Violet Love passed on an eiderdown that was too tattered for hotel guests. But I thank you for your concern."

He waves.

James rushes right over as soon as he sees me arrive. "I tried to stop him," he spits out, "but he was a big chap and he wasn't about to listen. I wasn't going to tell him which was your tent. Niko and Tom wouldn't tell either, but then he asked Bruce Stewart, who pointed it out. He didn't take anything. I watched and there was no way I would budge. He just went through your belongings and commented on what he recognized."

James's words all come out in a rush. After hearing them, I push back the loose end of my tarp. Buck had rummaged through everything. I let the tarp fall in place again. So if I don't show up at the hotel, he knows where to find me. No wonder he didn't care if he let me out of his sight. I sit down on a stump next to my cold campfire. It's getting dark and I have to be at work in an hour.

"It was that fellow Buck Brooks, wasn't it?"

I nod in reply to James. "I ran into him at the hotel." I then explain Buck's demand that I return and work his land or be accused of breaking the law.

James sits across from me. "Can't you just use reason with him? Can't you just tell him you're on your own now and responsible for yourself?"

I shake my head. "There's no reasoning with Buck Brooks. Besides, it's not as simple as that. He only sees the work that needs to be done, and I am still legally bound. If I don't go, he'll force me by law. I know he will. There's nothing to do but stand up to him on my own. Maybe if he sees that I can't be bullied—that I've grown some backbone since I left—maybe then he just won't want me around." My teeth feel close to chattering. I'm not certain what's plaguing me more—the drop in temperature or Buck Brooks.

I don't feel like eating, although James insists on making me a cup of tea. "It'll warm you up." He leaves to attend to his fire, returning with the kettle. "It's as cold as an icehouse tonight. Look at this, even the ground's crisping up." He demonstrates by crushing a clump of brittle quackgrass with his foot. James sits across from me, watching me sip my tea, scraping a small ridge of dirt with his boot.

"Do you remember Ling Yu?" I ask.

James frowns a little. "Who?"

"The Chinaman?"

He nods faintly in the dusk.

"I'm not going to end up like that."

"You mean with your throat slit by your own hand?" James makes a small spluttery sound. "Of course you're not going to end up like that."

"No, what I mean is, I'm not going to get in a position where I have no options. I heard of boys from the Home who ended up that same way. Poisoned or hung themselves because they couldn't see their way out of terrible circumstances."

James leans forward. "Charlie, there's always options. They may not always be staring you in the face. And you might have to make them for yourself, but you've always got a choice in how you live your life. The problem with those fellows you're talking about was they were too young to know the choices were there. Or they were too miserable and confused by the time they needed them to see what they were."

"What about Mr. Ling Yu's, then? What were his?"

"Ling Yu's options?" James ponders this a moment. "Well, okay, maybe he's a case where they ran out. But it wasn't for lack of trying, from what I heard."

Despite the tea, I can't stop shivering. I clasp the cup with both hands to draw in more warmth.

James suddenly brightens. "I'll tell you what—you take my coat. You haven't stopped shivering since you sat down, and I'm not going to need it. I've got the stove in my tent, and you'll be back before I leave for the mine."

James removes his heavy duck coat as he is speaking. He now wears only his flannel shirt in the chilly night air. He pushes the coat toward me.

"I can't do that. What if you need it later?"

"I'm not planning on going anywhere. Take it, Charlie. I'm insisting."

It suddenly occurs to me that this is James's way of apologizing for not preventing Buck from rooting through my tent. Not that he could have stopped him. So I stop refusing. I take his coat and pull it on. It hangs loosely on my skinny frame, but I haven't been so warm since I'd worn John's old mackinaw. "I truly appreciate it. I'll get it back to you first thing in the morning."

James collects his kettle before starting toward his tent. "Good luck to you, Charlie. Good luck sending Buck Brooks on his way once and for all. If you start losing your nerve, just keep in mind I'm counting on you to be my neighbor and kin."

I acknowledge him by raising a hand. I sit on the stump and finish my tea before starting back into Frank. I walk the familiar route, following the wagon trail once I pass the temporary miners' shacks. It's cold, but it's a clear, windless night. I head past Thornley's Shoe Shop—the lights are out—and the mine livery. I then pass the seven miners' cabins on Alberta Avenue. Standing on the bridge spanning Gold Creek, I look back to where I've come from. They are humble circumstances I'm living in—even more humble than what I had at the Brookses, if that's possible. But I have friends, which I've never had in my life. And now that I do, I don't want to go back to the way it was.

I will speak my mind to Buck Brooks, and if he isn't reasonable, I'll take my chances on him turning me in.

By eight o'clock there is little standing room at the bar. The miners play blackjack, while others from the construction camp stand around drinking, smoking and generally jawing about whatever comes into their minds. I overhear they're expecting a crew of 130 men the next day, coming in to finish laying the Grassy Mountain Railway line between Frank and Lille.

And there is Buck, in the midst of it all, sipping his whiskey, just fitting right in. He doesn't let on that he knows me, but he sure takes to ordering me around. He knows I won't refuse and risk jeopardizing my position, so he takes advantage of it. He likes to see me waiting on him the way it used to be. He has me running for drinks, then complains I've left grimy fingerprints on his glass. He misses the cuspidor on purpose, and he expects I should be right there every time he lights up a smoke.

By ten o'clock the lighter drinkers have gone home. The more dedicated ones are getting louder by the second. I've already learned their drinking won't end until they become insensible or get caught up in the heat of an argument and wind up in a brawl.

"Where's that skinny helper when a fellow needs a light?" Buck booms above the general din of the bar.

I set the tray of empty glasses I'm carrying on the counter and search for the tin of matches in my apron. Realizing it's empty, I look for another.

"Come on, you lazy limey, get yourself over here. I need a match! And bring me another drink while you're at it. This one's almost done."

This time Buck's demand silences a few voices; even a couple of the more raucous fellows turn. Buck fills his yap with his last dreg of whiskey. The fellows lose interest, turn away, and the noise level rises again.

I pocket the matches. Sam hands me another glass of whiskey to take to Buck. I'm attempting to make my way over to where he's standing when Evan Kostos lays a hand on my arm. "That fellow over there's been hounding you all night. If I were you, Charlie, I'd give him a little extra something for providing you with so much work."

"Like what?" I ask.

Evan Kostos doesn't say anything. Instead, he begins working his mouth. He spits a great wad of gob in the glass. I stare in horror at the chunk of phlegm swimming in the whiskey.

"Charlie Sutherland!"

There's nothing else to do. I walk across the floor, whirling the glass as quickly and carefully as I can to get the contents mixed before serving it to Buck. He tosses it back in one throw. "That's more like it. Now, light the end of your good uncle's cigar."

About an hour later, Rose May comes calling at the saloon. She invites fellows wanting a bit of fun to go with her. I'm relieved when Buck leaves for a romp at the sporting house, leaving me free of him for the time being. I am curious what Sam pulls him aside to tell him on his way out the door, but I'm distracted from the encounter by an urgent request from fellows wanting another round.

Just before midnight, Sam sends me outside for a breath of good air. Despite the chill it's good to clear my lungs, and I am comfortably warm in James's coat, so I take a walk along Dominion Avenue. I nod and say good evening to Constable Leard, who is making his rounds. I figure it might be wise to leave a good impression, particularly if I'm to be pulled up on a charge of desertion by Buck Brooks.

A couple of miners stroll past on their way to the mine for the night shift. I turn back toward the hotel. As I do, I hear the approach of an incoming train—the wheeze and pant of a Mogul engine laboring up an incline—a freight train climbing from Passburg on its way from Macleod. It's behind schedule owing to a snowstorm that I'd heard a fellow in the bar talking about.

After my lunch, I head to the laundering room. Now that I'm hidden away, I don't expect I'll have to face Buck again until morning. It will give me a couple of hours to think about what to say.

Maddie has told Violet about Buck arriving and what he's demanding. "Want me to deal with him for you, Charlie?" She cranks the handle of the mangle as she feeds a sheet through the rollers.

I have to smile. She's got her spirit back since Maddie started helping out. "No, that's okay," I tell her. "I've got to do this myself."

"Suit yourself, but I'm here if you need me. Remember that."

"Thank you, Violet. I will."

We go through the routine of boiling, stirring and pounding without much talking. The room seems hotter, steamier and smaller than it ever has. I can't seem to do anything right, particularly as the night gets further along. I dump too much bluing in the kettle, tingeing the sheets an off-color; then I overdo the starch in the next load.

"Charlie, by the time these dry out they'll be so stiff they'll take the hide off a buffalo. I'm sure Mr. Steeves will hear about it if his guests wake up without their skin. We're going to have to start all over again and wash this muck out of them. Goldarn it, you're causing me more work than you're worth tonight. Why don't you take over here at the mangle?"

As I start forward, I trip and fall over a washboard.

"On second thought, you're likely to end up mangling your own arm. I'll tell you what. This load is ready to hang. I think that's a safe-enough undertaking, considering your state."

I carry the load outside. It's still dark, but a few lights shine in the hotel windows. The night clerk must have already woken the guests catching the Spokane Flyer, so I figure it must be about four o'clock. I haven't heard the train yet, but it was probably also delayed by the snowstorm outside Macleod. After securing the last peg onto the line, I return to the steamy room.

Fifteen

April 29, 1903

We work quietly at our separate chores for the next ten minutes. The only sound interrupting Violet's splashing and paddling is the metal grind of a slow-moving train. Judging by the distance and the time of night, I know it to be the freight train on the mine spur, collecting coal cars at the tipple.

I set the iron on the stove and sit at the folding table. It's just about then I hear the most terrifying sound of my life: an earth-shattering explosion like two steam engines going full out and colliding. I don't know what else could explain the horrific noise that comes without warning in the middle of the night.

Violet is knocked off her feet at the same time as the chair goes out from under me. Everything that is loose dances across the tables and counters and crashes to the floor. Panes of glass rattle and explode, and the timbers of the hotel shudder.

"Lord, the end of the world has come!" Violet struggles to get on her feet while I run to the window. It's thick with frost. I take hold of Violet's elbow, help her up, and with her trailing after me, I tear down the hall.

Doors fly open and dazed people emerge in their nightdresses, some rubbing bumps on their heads. In the lobby, some are screaming there's been an explosion at the mine. Others are sure it could be nothing less than an earthquake or a volcanic eruption. I run from the lobby into the dark. The second I am outside, a mighty wind, frigidly cold, comes down on me, almost sweeping me off my feet. The thunderous roar comes from the east. It's the crashing and grinding of rocks churning down the mountainside. Sparks are flying, and flashes of fire light the early morning sky. Women are wailing, people clutch at their thin nightclothes, and I overhear several people echoing Violet's words that the end of the world has surely come.

The air is heavy with dust, and it's difficult to breathe as I start toward the eastern flats. Puddles that had existed in the road the night before are now frozen, making it hazardous to run. I left James's coat in the laundering room, so I pull my arms tight about my chest. I make my way to the end of Dominion Avenue and along the path through the clearing with others headed the same way. The bridge spanning Gold Creek has been knocked out, swept away in a tide of mud. Squinting through the dark and clouds of dust, we can see that the miners' cottages on Alberta Avenue have also been destroyed. Most are immersed in rubble and rock, while others have entirely disappeared. What remains of two of the cottages is on fire.

Without a thought for their own safety, the men around me wade into the creek. I follow them, fighting my way through the freezing water and mud. The first cottage we reach is off its foundation. Other than that, it seems to be standing whole. The six remaining homes are not so lucky. They are not much more than hulks of burning timber. Hearing cries for help, the men who first arrived dig into the mud and slime with their hands or whatever instruments they can find, searching feverishly in the dark.

I stand on the strange, uneven ground. In the first weak light of dawn, I peer into the clouds of powdered limestone hanging in the air. I cannot see more than ten feet in front of me, but as far as I can see, the wagon trail is obliterated. All I know is I have to find James.

While rescuers pull survivors from the wreckage behind me, I set off into the choking dust. Within twenty feet I've fallen so many times my trousers are shredded and my legs are bruised and bleeding. The rocks are hot from their plunge down the mountain, and some are so large I can't see over them. From the top of one as tall as I am, I pick out two dim lights flitting like fireflies somewhere in the distance. Lanterns. Because of the curtain of dust it's hard to judge just how far away they are. But it does give me a small amount of hope. I decide there is no point going much farther until I have a light to guide me. It's all unknown territory now, and I'm quickly getting turned around.

I suddenly think of Maddie!

Scrambling back across the rock, I once again wade through Gold Creek. Panicked people are now flooding into the streets. I am soaked through and freezing so that my teeth are chattering crazily by the time I arrive at the Loves' cottage. Violet had immediately run to her children after leaving the hotel. She is now trying to calm them as they whimper softly, clutching hold of her skirt.

Maddie is also trying to calm them. "Charlie! What's happened?"

"It's too dark. I can't see." I pant heavily from all my running, and I can't get ahold of my shivering. "It's Turtle Mountain. It looks like it's come down. I've got to get to James. Violet, can you lend me a lamp?"

Violet nods as she pulls me into the parlor. She returns after searching for some of Peter's clothes. "They'll be too big for you, but you'll come down with pneumonia if you parade around in those things. Put them on. I'll get you a lantern."

I'm not about to argue. I change into Peter's shirt and trousers, tying them with a piece of curtain cord to keep them about my waist. Peter is already out, trying to get a grip on what happened, to see if he can help out, even if he only has one foot. Maddie insists on coming with me to search for James.

Daylight is breaking as we make our way back to Dominion Avenue. Rock dust still hovers in the air, but it's now light enough to see the extent of the disaster we had heard only an hour and a half before. As we turn onto the main street, all eyes are directed toward Turtle Mountain. The face of the mountain is gone. Maddie and I stare at the once wooded slope—it is sheered right off and now only a raw wound of broken limestone remains.

I think we might have more luck crossing the railroad bridge up near the boarding house. But when we reach it we discover we can go no farther. The landslide has passed less than thirty feet from the building where a hundred miners live. We're looking over a massive ocean of rock that extends east as far as we can see. The mine, tipple, buildings, track and power plant are all buried beneath it. The Crow's Nest River is swiftly flooding, backing up into Gold Creek, forming a lake.

"The miners are lost," someone wails.

It is a terrifying and most depressing sight. The mine entrance is gone, and it's impossible to say how far under the rubble it lies. Even if they are able to uncover the entrance, it isn't likely the structure of the mine beneath could hold up under the mountain falling.

"No hope for those in the valley, either," cries another.

I start to climb the jagged rock.

"Charlie, there's no point." Maddie follows. "You can see it's true. How could anything survive this?"

"I saw lights," I tell her. "It could be him. Somehow, he could have escaped. Look at that." I point to an island of trees. The slide has flowed around on either side and left them standing. "Not everything got hit. I've got to see for myself."

It's very difficult climbing. Daylight is trying hard to break through the swirling clouds of powdered limestone. The boulders are sharp-edged and irregular in size, snapped off by some tremendous force, not softly worn away by time. They are very small or they are as large as the Brookses' pig shed. We have moved forward maybe a hundred feet, but we are already exhausted after climbing up and down many more.

Voices and the lanterns of searchers flicker across the valley floor. At times the clouds of dust part and I can see men at the foot of the mountain, a rescue team working to reach the mine entrance. It appears they are building a raft to cross the flooding river. I can see that some are searching among the rocks for timbers to lash together. If they manage to get across, they will then have to locate the entrance to the mine, and there is no way to know the depth of the rock they'll be digging through. From where I stand it seems futile to even try.

I hear a boulder bounce swiftly toward us. I grab Maddie at the same time as she reaches for me, and we quickly duck behind a large rock. It passes just to our right, a huge gray shadow in the rock dust, flying like a train car hurtling through the air.

"Charlie!"

I turn to see why Maddie is shrieking. She points to horse legs and other horse parts, torn off and strewn about between the rocks. I put my arm around her and tell her not to look. Pressing her face into my shoulder, she begins crying and shaking something awful. I can't say it is a very pleasant sight to see myself. And then I remember the mine livery and the more than fifty pit ponies.

"Francis! The livery. It's all under here too."

My eyes sting and my nose begins to drip. It takes me a minute or so to get myself under control. I do only because Maddie needs comforting. I urge her on. We cover a little more ground. A glowing lamp seems suspended in the air until we draw closer. A cloud of dust blows off. A man is standing behind it on top of a rock. "You young folks shouldn't be here."

The crash of another rock hitting the valley floor sounds close to us.

"I'm searching for my friend. A fellow by the name of James Tuttle. We were camped in the valley together with others, just past the miners' shacks."

The fellow with the lantern may be someone from Frank who I would recognize under normal circumstances, but not at that particular moment. His hair and face are thick with dust. Even as he stands there, it continues to accumulate as if it's blowing off a fire and he's standing upwind. His lantern flickers. Solemnly he shakes his head. "If there was a camp, there's nothing left of it. Everything's buried from here for a mile east. I've been over it. Not a soul could have survived this catastrophe."

"But I saw two lights," I desperately argue, "not long after it happened. Out here somewhere. I was looking from the direction of the wagon trail by Gold Creek. It could have been James or others from the camp."

"No." He shakes his head. "It wasn't. I can guarantee. You most probably saw Sid Choquette's light. He was the only fellow out here. He's a railroad man, a brakeman. Soon after the mountain came down, he set off across this heap. He made it all the way to the track on the east side of it and stopped the Spokane Flyer. Waved it down before it collided with the rock. Sid's a brave fellow. He saved a load of lives by risking his own and doing what he did. Now, you two go back to town. There's nothing to find and it's dangerous to be walking about. This whole area will soon be flooded. I'm very sorry about your friend."

I can't move. Like the fellows searching for the entrance to the mine, I can't just give up looking, no matter how pointless it seems. But Maddie is tugging at my arm. "Charlie, he's right. There are men searching. If James is alive, they'll find him. Let's go back and wait for word."

I turn around. I tell myself they will find him and that this fellow could not possibly have covered the entire valley himself. James is smart. He has so much to look forward to. He wouldn't have just gone and got himself killed. "Maybe he got out before it came down. Maybe he heard it coming."

"Maybe," Maddie says.

We start back over the rocks, stepping across trees snapped like matches, twisted metal, a rail from the mine track. And everywhere there is mud seeping around the rocks.

"Maddie, I'm going back to the hotel. If there's word, that's where I'll hear it. You go back to Violet's. I'll come get you when I know."

She agrees. I watch her start through the crowded streets. I then head for the Imperial Hotel, passing folks piling their belongings into wagons, wanting to get out of town. They have decided they will be safer in Blairmore. They point to another outcrop of rock hanging above Frank, certain it will also come down.

By mid-morning the bar in the hotel is busier than on a Saturday night after payday. Men come in with the hope of hearing news and to discuss what's being done. Some toss back whiskey, intent on calming their nerves. Mr. Steeves asks if I can help out in the barroom, suggesting that it might be better for me to keep busy; it will help occupy my thoughts while I wait for word of James.

More terrible news comes in while I'm clearing glasses. It is of the homes on Alberta Avenue, which were all directly in the path of the landslide. Mr. Alex Leitch and his wife, along with two of their boys, have been found dead, buried beneath their home. Another two boys are missing, but their three daughters are alive. Mr. Alex Clark's entire family, with the exception of his daughter, who was working at the boarding house, is said to be lost. The last house on Alberta Avenue, the Clark home, is buried and gone. Mr. Clark is one of the miners trapped in the mine.

Early in the afternoon, one of the fellows who is aiding in the search comes in with further news. Thornley's Shoe Shop is plowed under, but by a quirk of good fortune, Mr. Thornley had stayed overnight in Frank and his life was saved. The mine livery is buried beneath the rock. I listen closely when I hear mention of Francis. "We found Francis Rochette. Poor fellow was lying in the rocks like he'd stretched out for a nap, but he was dead."

My throat tightens and my stomach knots up. I excuse myself and tear down to the closet in the laundering room. It takes some minutes to get myself together. I look at the window. The frost is now melted and dripping down the pane. I think of Francis and how the last thing he said was how he'd have to break ice for the horses in the morning. Now Francis is gone and those horses lie in bits among the rocks. I suddenly have to see Cody.

Mr. McDonald's livery stable is sound as ever, and so is my horse. Cody is appreciative of the big helping of oats I suddenly have the notion to feed him. While he chews happily, spitting out the straw, I glance at the row of stalls set aside for the hotel guests. I ask the livery hand what has happened to the gray shire.

"That fellow who owned him—he was one of the first to beat it out of here this morning. A big fellow with a mangy beard. He came and got his horse, said he was getting out of here and that we were all crazy to want to be living beneath a mountain. When I asked if he wasn't going to join in the searching, he just cussed at me and rode off." The livery hand shrugs. "I say good riddance to him. Don't know what kind of help a fellow like that would be anyhow."

I know exactly what kind of help Buck Brooks would be. Absolutely none at all. After I've reassured myself that Cody's in good health, I return to the hotel. More rescue workers are coming in to rest up, telling stories of what they've seen. Mr. John McVeigh and the entire construction camp working on the Grassy Mountain Railway are buried, along with a mile of the Canadian Pacific Railway. Mr. James Graham, his wife, two sons and the two Indians who worked on his dairy farm have also lost their lives. It's believed that all those living in the miners' temporary dwellings scattered across the eastern flats were buried in the slide.

A man of about forty, the backs of his hands scraped up and his face stained with sweat and dust from working in the rock, stands with the group gathered at the bar. "The old trapper, Andy Grissack," he tells another, "they found him wrapped in his tent still clutching his frying pan. When the men turned him over, his scalp came away like a husk."

For the tenth time that morning I blink tears from my eyes. I wonder if old Andy had got too close to the Lemon Mine, never believing its curse. I imagine him with his gear hanging about his waist, frying his breakfast before setting out to check his traps. He would never have known what hit him. Or maybe he would have realized it in the last split second, seeing as how he was so attuned to the mountain where he lived.

I break through the knot of men. "What about the fellows camping? The ones between the river and the miners' shacks? Has there been any word?"

A few men turn. "What fellows are you talking about, lad?" The question is asked by a smartly dressed man in a gray bowler and black frock coat. I don't recognize him as someone I've seen around Frank. I guess he must be the superintendent or the manager of something important—come to see what's happened after hearing news of the slide.

"There was Mr. Tom Roberts, Niko the Finn and Evan Kostos. They all worked at the mine. Others camping in the valley were without work, but they were looking for it."

The fellow in the snappy bowler hat turns his head and sniffs. "I don't recognize any of those names as men I would know."

The rest of the men simply shrug, except for the youngest of the group, who lays his hand on my arm and leans toward me. When he speaks, it's in a lowered voice. "Sometimes folks like that prefer to keep to themselves. Particularly if their origins make them a similar sort."

I'm not sure if he's talking about the man in the bowler or the fellows in the camp. It dawns on me he means Niko and Evan. He means Tom, Ling Yu and me. We are all a similar sort.

The man with the scrapes on his hands explains. "There're always men moving through here looking for work. It would be a terrible twist of fate if some had chosen to pitch their tents beneath the mountain last night. But if they did, they'd be a long way under the rock. There's not a thing any of us can do to help them now."

It's then I realize I am the only one looking for James.

Sixteen

It's late afternoon and it will soon be growing dark. I grab James's coat and tell Mr. Steeves he'll have to do without me for a time. I have some searching of my own to do. He doesn't pay me much attention, though, as his gaze is fastened out the window. Coming down Dominion Avenue is the night shift, the trapped miners, worn out and bedraggled, looking like walking dead men. Cries of disbelief, cheers and toasts ring out in the barroom.

I stop in the road just long enough to hear how they managed to still be alive.

The miners heard the roar and felt the blast shake the earth like everyone else. At the moment of the slide, wind rushed through the tunnels, blowing out their lamps and throwing them against the walls. Working at their separate locations, they immediately began to make their way to the mine portal. They discovered it blocked with fallen timber and rock. It would be an impossible task to move the debris with the tools they had, particularly when they had no idea how far they would have to dig.

The lower tunnel was filling with water. Knowing their air supply would soon be cut off, they climbed through a manway into a coal chamber. Gas was accumulating quickly and their time was running out. It was then one fellow recalled a particular coal seam, an outcrop running to the surface of the mountain. They began to dig their way through the coal. Hours later, worn and exhausted, they broke through the surface. Seventeen of the twenty miners were now coming down the street. Three other men were not so lucky. They had been sitting outside the mine entrance on their dinner break when the slide hit. All three were swept away in the rock. One of those was Mr. Clark, whose cottage on Alberta Avenue had been swallowed up with all but one of his daughters inside.

I wish for my own miracle as I set out across the swelling limestone sea. Boulders still tumble down Turtle Mountain at random, so I have to be alert. The river has backed up so that it now forms a lake. It covers the area where the tipple, mine buildings and power plant had once stood. With all the landmarks gone it's hard to be sure, but I head in the direction I know the camp to be.

Through the lingering dust, I pick out figures clambering over the rocks. They are still searching for bodies or anyone too injured to move, listening for cries for help. I climb to the top of a boulder the height of a hayloft. From here I have a much better view of the slide and the path it took. After breaking off and sweeping down the mountain, it spread across the valley, spilling in a fan shape far up the slope on the other side. It was the air from high up that froze everything. This had been the theory of some fellows discussing it in the bar, but I can now see how it makes sense. The mass of rocks plowing down the mountainside had brought with it the frozen air from 5,000 feet, forcing the warmer air out of the valley.

I continue to make my way across the rock, turning around often to gauge how far I've come. The slide is bordered by Gold Creek at its western edge. I scramble over the rock for close to two hours. As time drags on and I become wearier, I begin catching the toes of my boots and tripping more often. I miscalculate jumps between larger rocks, fall hard several times and whack my shins on the sharp edges of the boulders. My clothes are muddy and torn; my skin is bruised, scraped and bleeding. My nose and eyes burn with the limestone dust when I finally sink to a rock.

I have to admit I have come at least as far as where the camp should have been. Maybe even much farther—probably I passed back and forth over it and have been walking in circles. But considering how close it had been to the river, and seeing how the whole area is flooded, there is also a good chance it's now beneath the lake.

There isn't going to be a miracle for James. There isn't going to be a miracle for any of the men camped in the valley who had come to the North-West Territories with hopes of a better life. They had left their kin at home until they got settled and could provide the comforts children and women need. Now they lie beneath the rock while their families carry on, not knowing their fate. Of course, there are some who'd come wandering through on their own, and they might never be missed. That's just as sorrowful a thought.

I'm thinking all these things, trying to hold on to my grief, when—at a distance—I spot something in the rocks. Under a sky that is now growing quite dark, I make my way over to whatever it is. I have to climb high to reach what's wedged between a giant boulder and a smaller rock. I wrestle with the object, a battered, flattened piece of forged metal. Perhaps it's something from the blacksmith's. When it finally gives, I fall backward, whacking the metal against the rock with a scraping sound. I turn it over in my hand. It's blackened at one end, and all that's identifiable is a spout. A coffee pot.

For a moment I just stare at what's left of that coffee pot. Then, in the next few minutes, all the lonesomeness I've felt since losing my brother Jack comes tumbling out as forceful as the slide itself. I can't keep it trapped in any longer. I feel more helpless than I have in my entire life. I'm angry at everything: at Jack for abandoning me, at the Home for sending me to this horrible place called Canada, at Buck and Albert for mistreating me the way they did. I'm furious at James for being my friend and getting my hopes raised for a decent future and then going and getting himself killed! I want to punch something, but with nothing but rock around to punch, I'd break my hand if I did.

I go on wailing for some time until there doesn't seem much point in going on any longer. If I haven't succeeded in raising the fellows I'd come to know as my friends with my caterwauling by then, it isn't likely I will. I wipe my face on the back of my sleeve. The rock dust mucks in with my tears so my cheeks feel tight, like they're smeared with wall plaster.

I sniff again and concentrate on pulling myself together. There's nothing to do but head back toward the lights of town. I wedge the coffee pot back between the rocks, thinking that, someday, someone else might be searching for answers. Maybe it will explain something to them. I start back toward Gold Creek. As I make my way across the slide, I feel like I'm dragging my heart strapped to my boot, hauling it behind me like one of the broken rocks.

It's strange to hear water lapping at the shores of a lake so close by. The cool woods of jackpine, poplars and lupines are gone, and ahead of me is only a desert of rock. I don't know this place any longer. I won't be staying. There's nothing to keep me, and I have only Cody left.

There is still much confusion on the streets. Folks chatter, exchange stories or bits of information as they load belongings into wagons or wheelbarrows. I overhear one fellow tell another that one of the mine tipples was found a mile away. Rails had been discovered twisted like licorice at the furthermost reaches of the slide. A woman is wailing because the cemetery is buried in rock, so how can they give a fitting interment to the dead folk? An older lad tells of Mr. Clark, who had been eating his dinner when the slide struck, and how his body was found a quarter of a mile away from the mine.

People continue to wander down the railroad track toward Blairmore, dazed, carrying what must have seemed important to grab hold of in their confusion: a soup ladle or a sack full of mending.

Mr. Steeves kindly offers me a room at the hotel for the night. Maddie comes by, but I don't feel much like visiting. I tell her I'll come see her in the morning, after everything that has happened has had a chance to settle in my mind. I pick up a bit of soup in the dining room, then retire to my room to wash before returning to the barroom.

It's a simple room with a bed, washstand, chair and table. I pour water into the basin before pulling James's coat off and tossing it over the chair. Something falls to the floor: a long, narrow pocketbook. Sitting on the edge of the bed, I bend to pick it up. I run my hand across the rugged leather. It was important to James or he wouldn't have stored it in his pocket. I untie the knot binding it up.

A number of papers and folded documents fall out: James's bank book issued by the Union Bank, a letter of credit from the same bank in Winnipeg to another in St. Albert, and an amount of cash. The last paper I unfold is the Dominion land office receipt for ten dollars, attached to an official agreement for James Tuttle to prove up 160 acres within three years. The directions give its location as just north of Edmonton near the village of St. Albert.

I'm not sure how long I stare at these documents, shuffling through them, reading every word, hardly aware of taking a breath. Finally I tie them all together and return them to the pocket of his coat. I wash the rock dust from my face and hands, as I've come to the room to do, before returning to the barroom to work for Sam.

I try to keep my thoughts under control by concentrating on my work. I've heard many of the stories flying about the room, and some I haven't heard. But my mind is too occupied with those in the valley, who were close to me, to stop and listen in, or to be blanked out by keeping busy.

When I finally collapse, I can hardly sleep for all that I'm feeling. For the longest time I can't control the fits of bawling. I keep seeing James in my mind, and I can't believe he's gone. I see the other fellows, all used to working in dangerous circumstances—quick to risk their lives for others—now all crushed beneath the rock. I go on like this for what must be hours because when I've finally wrung all the tears out, the moon is starting to fade as dawn begins.

I then begin tossing over and over what I'm going to do from here. I remember something James said. It was when Buck showed up and there seemed no way out for me.

Charlie, there's always options. They may not always be staring you in the face. And you might have to make them for yourself, but you've always got a choice in how you live your life.

I picture James sitting across from me by the fire, telling me this. I imagine him looking back and discussing it in light of his own death. I imagine him advising me, knowing that once he'd got over the shock of his passing, he'd be as direct and straightforward as he'd been about Ling Yu's demise.

He'd say that the terrible thing that happened to him had just happened, and there was no way of changing it. It was an accumulation of coincidences and unlucky occurrences, as it was with Ling Yu. It was fate. He'd then go on to say, "But if you think about it, you're fortunate, and not just because you have your life. I've left you an opportunity, and Charlie—you'd be a fool to pass it up."

I sit up in bed with my mind racing. I now focus on what I've been afraid to think about since I came across the pocketbook.

I think of James and how he'd come from circumstances the same as my own. I think of his time spent in foster homes and how he'd gone to the industrial school. He'd be fiercely disappointed to learn the land and the future he'd worked so hard for had passed back to the land office and into the hands of a stranger. I knew him—maybe not for long, but I knew how much his accomplishments meant to him.

I'd be letting him down if I didn't at least make an effort to work his land. James would expect that I wouldn't just quit. He'd want me to use the opportunity he'd left me to show that chaps like us—and of a similar sort—could do it. Despite all else, we could prove up. He'd come so close to doing it himself. In a way, we'd still be doing it together.

And if I took on the responsibility of working his land, I could still go by my Christian name of Charlie. I'd just say it was my middle name, James Charlie Tuttle, and I'd always been known by it to distinguish me from my dad. Besides, the name isn't of much consequence. As Mr. Wittecombe had once told me, it's not the name that's important; it's what a boy makes of what's inside.

I now can't sleep for excitement and fear of what I've made up my mind to do.

Just after daybreak, I walk into the barroom where Sam is already preparing for the day. I stand at the bar. Sam looks at me in a puzzled way.

"A shot of Arbuckles," I tell him.

Sam smiles. "Yes, sir, whatever you say." He pours me a mug of the strong, black coffee. "Yesterday was a tough day on you, Charlie, what with losing your home and your friend." He passes me a biscuit along with the coffee.

I hold up my mug. "To my birthday tomorrow. May first."

"Well, I'll drink to that." Sam pours a mug of coffee for himself. He clinks his cup to mine. "Best wishes on your birthday. And how many will that be?"

"Eighteen," I tell him.

I hope it's come out convincing. I would really only be seventeen, and I might not even be that considering it isn't my true birthday. It was the one bestowed on me by Mr. Wittecombe at the Home.

"Eighteen," he muses, smacking his lips. "A fine age."

I nod. Yes, all considered, it is a fine age.

Sam begins polishing a tray of glasses. "Say, did that big fellow—the one that was in here bullying you the other night—did he ever come back?"

I know he has to mean Buck. I shake my head. "No, he left town."

"Good." Sam inspects the glass he's just polished by holding it up to the light. "I told him I didn't welcome the business of anyone who abuses my employees, particularly those that work as hard as you. But I generally don't expect his type to listen."

So that's what Sam had pulled Buck aside to say. I begin thinking maybe it wasn't just the slide that drove Buck out. Maybe after what Sam said, Buck saw things were different, and it struck him they could never go back to being the way they were. It's difficult to tell Sam what I've really come to say after hearing him describe me like that. But I've got to do it.

"There's something else I've got to tell you, Sam. I've got to say goodbye. I'm on my way now, but I want you to know I appreciate all you've done."

Sam's smile fades. But I don't think it's just me saying goodbye. I think it's the effects of the calamity and the accumulation of the tragic stories and losses. "This whole thing has put everyone on edge, and I think we're all thinking this may not be the place to be. But I don't blame you for getting out before you set down roots. I'll be sorry to see you go, but all the best to you, Charlie. You've been a good employee here."

I step onto the street wearing James's coat with the pocketbook stowed safely inside. Dust is still settling and the occasional rock still bounces down the mountain as I walk toward Mr. McDonald's Livery. At the end of the street, passengers from the train have just arrived. The CPR has come as far west as it could before it was stopped by the slide. The passengers had no choice but to disembark and cover the final stretch into Frank on foot, hauling their carpetbags over two miles of rock. Weary and confused by the unusual circumstances of their journey, they now stand on the platform, waiting for another train so they might continue west.

I collect West Coast Cody at the livery. I then set out for Violet Love's cottage, my last stop before heading out of Frank. On my way, I think that maybe, someday, I'll find Mr. Longhurst and pay him for my horse. Perhaps once I've harvested my first crop.

We trot up the street toward the Loves' cottage. Standing outside, Cody snorts and his hoof scrapes the earth. Violet and Maddie, accompanied by a swarm of children, come to the front yard. Violet plunks her hands on her hips; the look she's wearing asks me what I'm up to.

"I'm off to work James's land, Violet. I've got a lot to do if I'm going to prove up in three years." I then explain how I'd spent the evening considering what James had said. "It's what he would have wanted, and I learned that I'm capable from the fellows in the camp. I can't pass up the opportunity. Especially when not so many chances have come along in my life."

When it sinks into Violet's head that I'm leaving, she begins twisting her apron in her hands. She says she wishes I wouldn't go and that she would be very pleased if I'd consider staying. I'd have to share her affections with all her other children, but she has plenty to go around.

I smile, thinking how things might have been if I'd run into Violet ten years earlier. I then tell her I'm too grown up for that. But so she doesn't take it that I don't appreciate the offer, I say, "But I did lose some friends in the slide. I sure could use another."

Violet says she'd be delighted to be my friend. She then goes on to tell me that I'm certain to come across more people like James and the others in the camp. "You'll find out as life goes along that most folks aren't like the Brookses."

I nod. I then look at Maddie, standing quietly off to the side. A small boy whimpers and tugs at her skirt, and I think back to the first time I'd seen her, looking so pretty, sitting by the campfire in her buckskin dress, working at her quilling in between tending the smoking deer meat. I then think of something Roly had said. It was when he was talking about asking Olivia for her hand in marriage, and how he wanted a wife who was warm and kind. He also wanted a wife who knew what to expect. "Someone who's not going to hightail it out of here the first time she gets a blackfly bite or gets whomped on the head with a nugget of hail." I remember what he'd said about a man not being able to do it on his own. He'd seen the results.

"Maddie," I say, "I'll be back in the fall. I'll need to work the winter months for supplies. I'm going to try to get on at one of the mines in the pass. Will you still be here?"

Violet pulls her close. "Of course she will."

Maddie smiles. Her future is as uncertain as my own, yet she's reassuring when she pats the head of the child clutching her knees. I know Violet will look after her well.

"I'll write to you," I tell her.

Maddie suddenly removes the beaded neckband she wears, brings it to Cody's side and ties it around my wrist. I thank her.

"You go now, Charlie," Violet Love tells me. "You go sink your plow into the earth, and you write and tell us if the soil is good."

My heart is thumping wildly. I have no idea where the courage to strike out and do what I'm about to do has come from. I suppose part of it might be having learned that what Violet said is right; most folks aren't like Buck and Albert. On the other hand, maybe it's been there all along—maybe it was deep down, waiting to surface when all other things were just right. Like the final cold snap that combined with all other existing forces and caused Turtle Mountain to walk.

But right now, all I really know for certain is I owe it to James and those like him. I tip my cap and start Cody toward the trail heading north.

Acknowledgements

I am fortunate to have family, friends and colleagues who make the writing process so much easier simply by providing support in the many ways that they do. I am grateful to all of you. There are a number of people in particular, however, who I must thank individually as they contributed directly to the writing of this book.

First of all, my sincere gratitude goes to Jake Valli for sharing the invaluable letter from Dr. Barnardo's Home regarding his great-grandmother's history. She was truly an inspirational lady.

I am grateful to my dear friend Gloria Luthe, who hails from "the Smoke," for her critical eye, and to Keith Gilroyed and Bill Talbot for their individual contributions.

My deep appreciation goes to Dr. Shaun Haines, Ojibway-Cree Metis elder. Thank you, Shaun, for the song, and most of all for giving me a much greater insight into aboriginal life in Canada.

As well, I am indebted to Wendy Walker, Cree-Mi'k Ma'k Métis Pipe Carrier and Ceremonial Leader, again for the insight and thoughtful advice.

And finally, to my husband, Jeff, who has a deep interest in western Canadian history and was as excited about the potential for this story as I was. Thanks, Jeff, for driving thousands of miles to traipse through museums and visit coal mines without one word of complaint. But that's just like you.

Also of tremendous help were the following organizations, which work so hard to keep their local histories alive: the Frank Slide Interpretive Center (Frank, Alberta), Kootenai Brown Pioneer Village (Pincher Creek, Alberta), Museum of the North-West Mounted Police (Fort Macleod, Alberta), Coleman Museum (Coleman, Alberta), Hillcrest Coal Mine (Hillcrest, Aberta), Atlas Coal Mine (Drumheller, Alberta), Fort Edmonton Park (Edmonton, Alberta), the Provincial Archives of Alberta, and historic Virginia City, Montana.

Historical Note

At the beginning of the twentieth century, the mining town of Frank sat just east of the Crow's Nest Pass at the foot of Turtle Mountain. Most of the inhabitants were asleep at 4:10 AM on April 29, 1903, when the north face of the mountain collapsed. It took only one hundred seconds for ninety million tons of limestone to sweep through the valley, leveling houses, shacks and tents. Once the choking white clouds of limestone cleared, the official death count stood at seventy-six persons.

But no one knows for certain how many people really perished, for another fifty or so men were said to be living in tents in the valley as they looked for work. If so, these transient workers would have died along with the townsfolk in the most catastrophic landslide in the recorded history of the Rocky Mountains.

A Note on the Barnardo Homes

   In the mid-nineteenth century, thousands of destitute children lived in London's East End. After years of rampant unemployment, sparked, in part, by the Industrial Revolution, poverty-stricken parents, broken in spirit, abandoned their children to fend for themselves. These homeless children often banded together, scavenging, stealing and begging for food. At night they curled up in the rat-infested alleys to sleep. The only goal of their poor, day-to-day existence was to stay alive.

  Toward the end of the century a new social conscience emerged. Charitable organizations and individuals reached out to the impoverished. Thomas John Barnardo was one of these individuals. Born in Dublin on July 4, 1845, he was to become "father" to thousands of Great Britain's homeless and abandoned children.

  Dr. Barnardo opened his first home for children in London's East End. He immediately realized the need for a larger residence when he was flooded with children needing a meal and a warm place to sleep. In 1870, he purchased Stepney Causeway, a large building in the East End of London. Children were not only provided with a home, which they helped to maintain; they were also trained in domestic chores and trades, and they attended a school on the premises. Within ten years, Dr. Barnardo's homes were caring for more children than any other agency.

  When Barnardo first opened his doors, most of the children were "street arabs," boys and girls with no known relatives. But with no social agencies at the time, financially destitute single parents and relatives soon began to admit their children to the homes.

  Thomas Barnardo was initially reluctant to follow the trend of other organizations and send his children to Canada. He was particularly sensitive to Canadian claims that Great Britain was dumping its "street urchins" on Canada's soil. But he was persuaded by the fact that Canada needed young emigrants to serve as laborers and domestics. Britain's cities were overpopulated. Barnardo believed the children would have a much richer life in Canada than in the British Isles. So in 1869, with some trepidation, he allowed a few of his boys to accompany Miss Annie MacPherson's children. Miss MacPherson ran a children's agency of her own. When he was assured the emigration was successful, he sent a hundred Barnardo boys between the ages of fourteen and seventeen to Canada.

Selection of the children who would participate in the "great Canadian adventure" was very stringent. Children were considered on the basis of a physical examination, their character and their completion of some basic English education, as well as training in domestics or a trade. The successful children were each supplied with a "Canadian Outfit": a Barnardo trunk containing specified articles of clothing, a Bible, a hymn book, a copy of *The Pilgrim's Progress* and *The Traveler's Guide*. They also carried a travel bag with their Barnardo number, destination and landing card. On the day of departure, with much fanfare—the Barnardo band playing and the Red Ensign of Canada flying—the children embarked on their voyage.

As railway expansion progressed west and the prairies opened for settlement, there was a great demand for farm laborers and domestic help. Barnardo believed deeply that this was an enormous opportunity for the children to contribute to the development of the new land. In 1896, he opened the Winnipeg Distributing and Receiving Home for boys and girls heading to the western dominions. Children between the ages of eight and thirteen passed through this center.

Homesteaders wanting the services of a Barnardo boy or girl applied to the Home. By the terms of the agreement, the employer was to provide the child with sufficient room and board in exchange for farm labor. Employers were also to ensure the children attended school. At fourteen, however, school became optional, and the child was expected to negotiate a wage for labor. These wages were to be remitted to the Bank of Commerce, where each child was issued a bank account. A pass book was sent to the child, although no withdrawals could be made without permission of the Home until they were eighteen.

The most important feature of Barnardo's colonization scheme was the Industrial Farm for Barnardo Boys near Russell, Manitoba. There, boys aged seventeen to twenty were trained in all areas of agriculture and farm operation in order to prepare them for homesteading. At the end of an eight-month apprenticeship they were eligible to begin frontier life. Young men deemed suitable received a parcel of 160 acres, which the Canadian government offered to all immigrants over eighteen years. The land office also outfitted each Barnardo settler with an ox, plow, cart, harness and provisions to start his homestead. Additional implements, stock, seed and building materials were available to them at reduced costs.

Dr. Barnardo's Industrial Farm closed in 1904, and the Winnipeg Distributing and Receiving Home in 1918, although emigration of British children continued. The final emigration of Barnardo children was in 1939. In all, more than 30,000 Barnardo children emigrated from Great Britain to Canada between the years 1882 and 1939.

Thomas Barnardo and the members of his foundation worked hard to better the lives of thousands of children, and for this, their efforts and intentions can only be admired. But sadly, in Canada, the children were often viewed by their employers as nothing more than cheap, accessible labor. Many were expected to work very hard from early dawn until late at night, chopping wood, caring for animals and working in the fields. Often they were given tasks far beyond their physical strength. If they did not perform their chores correctly, or if they were just not strong or fast enough, they were subjected to beatings and other brutal punishments. Already isolated, scattered on farms across a country as vast as Canada, many lived in misery and fear. In some cases the emotional and physical abuse drove the children to run away, or even to suicide. Running away was rarely successful given the enormous distances and severe climate.

The children also had to contend with prejudices and ignorant attitudes. They were considered cast-offs, not wanted in their own country, criminals who would have a bad influence on Canadian youth. To be called a "Home Child" was a derogatory thing. The children were sometimes accused of crimes they didn't commit, and in school they were often ridiculed for their accents and ignorance of Canadian ways.

Today, we know just how essential self-esteem, a sense of belonging, and unconditional love are to a healthy childhood. Given their backgrounds and the enormous hardships they came up against, we have to admire the resilience and strength of spirit of these young immigrants, who overcame it all to become Canada's successful farmers, businessmen and professionals.

Although this is a fictional story, I sincerely hope it does justice to them.

Katherine Holubitsky
January 2005

Also by Katherine Holubitsky

Alone at Ninety Foot

Thoughtful, full of passion, often funny and sometimes tearful, fourteen-year-old Pamela Collins is struggling to come to terms with the emotional overload that her mother's death has brought to her life.

"My reaction, right from page one of *Alone at Ninety Foot*, was this is good, this is really good. Holubitsky draws the characters with confidence and authenticity of a writer in tune with today's teens. Pam Collins, the protagonist, is fresh and vivid and very believable. It's a book written from the heart—guaranteed to make you smile, chuckle, and you may even shed a tear."

—Julie Johnston, two-time
Governor General's Award winner

CLA Book of the Year for Young Adults
IODE Violet Downey Book Award Winner
ALA/YALSA Best Books for Young Adults—2000
Pick of the Lists—American Booksellers Association
New York Public Library Books for the Teen Age
Canadian Children's Book Center Our Choice Starred selection

1-55143-204-8

Also by Katherine Holubitsky

Last Summer in Agatha

When Rachael meets Michael, the attraction is mutual and immediate, and the boring summer she's been anticipating in dusty Agatha suddenly appears promising. But then her new beau's painful past begins to get in the way. Michael's life has been torn apart by the death two years earlier of the older brother he idolized. Despite his affection for Rachel, he can no longer hold his frustration and anger inside and he begins to strike out at the people around him.

For years Michael and his friend Scott have been at odds with Cory and Taylor. In the past the four boys amused themselves by exchanging insults. But this summer things begin to spin out of control, and Rachel finds herself caught in the middle of a series of increasingly violent pranks that threaten the stability of the small community and force her to question the boundaries of friendship and trust.

R. Ross Annett Award for Children's Literature 2002

"...strong and powerfully written. Holubitsky makes you taste the dust of southern Alberta, feel the heat of the prairie sun, and live the lazy rhythm of small-town life. Highly Recommended." —*Canadian Materials (VIII/#3)*

1-55143-190-4

Also by Katherine Holubitsky

The Hippie House

Summer 1970. Emma Jenkins is fourteen years old and looking forward to entering her first year of high school. It is a time of idealistic freedom and experimentation for Emma, her cousin Megan, and the young people of Pike Creek. While her brother Eric's band practices in what Uncle Pat has dubbed the Hippie House, the girls suntan on their small lake and hitchhike into town to hang around the drop-in center. They find the growing crowd of long-haired musicians and hangers-on that begin to show up at the farm both enticing and a bit scary.

The beginning of the school year brings excitement and change. But when eighteen-year-old Katie Russell disappears, Emma's teenage sense of immortality is suddenly shattered. A month later, when Eric discovers Katie's body in the Hippie House, now abandoned for the winter, the entire community is thrown into turmoil.

"…absorbing and thoughtful…" —*VOYA*

"…This outstanding coming of age story should be in every high school library…" —*Resource Links*

"…Holubitsky's strengths—her emotional perceptiveness, her graceful, nuanced writing, her painfully true depictions of teen life—shine here…" —*Quill & Quire*

1-55143-316-8